A GOOD GIRL & A DOWN SOUTH MILLIONAIRE 3

MICHELLE ELAINE

Cole Hart
SIGNATURE NOVELS

A Good Girl & A Down South Millionaire 3

Copyright © 2020 by Michelle Elaine

All rights reserved.

Published in the United States of America.

All rights reserved. No part of this publication may be reproduced, distributed, or transmitted in any form or by any means, including photocopying, recording, or other electronic or mechanical methods, without the prior written permission of the publisher, except in the case of brief quotations embodied in critical reviews and certain other noncommercial uses permitted by copyright law. For permission requests, please contact: www.colehartsignature.com

This is a work of fiction. Names, characters, places, and incidents either are the products of the author's imagination or are used fictitiously. Any resemblance of actual persons, living or dead, businesses, companies, events, or locales is entirely coincidental. The publisher does not have any control and does not assume any responsibility for author or third-party websites or their content.

The unauthorized reproduction or distribution of this copyrighted work is a crime punishable by law. No part of the book may be scanned, uploaded to or downloaded from file sharing sites, or distributed in any other way via the Internet or any other means, electronic, or print, without the publisher's permission. Criminal copyright infringement, including infringement without monetary gain, is investigated by the FBI and is punishable by up to five years in federal prison and a fine of $250,000 (www.fbi.gov/ipr/).

This book is licensed for your personal enjoyment only. Thank you for respecting the author's work.

Published by Cole Hart Signature, LLC.

Mailing List

To stay up to date on new releases, plus get information on contests, sneak peeks, and more,

Go To The Website Below...

www.colehartsignature.com

PROLOGUE

JULIAN

$\mathcal{I}$ stood in the hall looking into the hospital room through a window. Besides the few people walking up and down the hallway, the intensive care unit was relatively quiet, but I could hardly focus anyway. For several minutes I stared blankly ahead into the room, completely zoned out. I wasn't thinking about the heart monitor and the various tubes and wires running in every direction. Instead, I was wondering how in the hell things had gotten to this point. For nearly two years I felt like I was trapped in a nightmare. I was ready to wake up. In the meantime, I would settle for seeing my daughter open her eyes.

I heard the clicking sound of her heels before I saw Sophia Mercer appear at my side. She gently placed her hand on my shoulder in what was intended to be a calming gesture. However, nothing within my soul was calm. I wasn't sure if I would ever feel peace again.

"Julian, you probably should not be here alone," she said, her eyes darting around the hallway. "I spoke to Lucas just yesterday. We still don't know where Michaela is."

Within my peripheral vision, I could see the two large men standing a few yards away – Sophia's security detail. Due to recent events, I was not surprised that Manny Mercer insisted on his wife not traveling alone. I turned to look Sophia directly in the eyes. I was sure that the stress of the last several weeks was showing on my face.

"Fuck Michaela Pitt," I said through gritted teeth. "She's the reason we're standing here in the first place. She's the reason for all this shit. She's the reason my child is lying in that hospital bed unconscious, connected to all types of machines and shit. She's the reason my grandchild had a traumatic birth. She's the reason Aaron ..."

Sophia shook her head and raised her hands to stop me from speaking any further. "Julian, I am very well aware of the damage that Michaela has caused to both our families. However, you know that you were her original target. I don't think that has changed just because of what she has done to our children. You still need to make sure that you are watching your back."

"Sophia, we've known each other over thirty years. You should know me better than that. I've got men all through this hospital ... 24/7. Just because you don't see them doesn't mean that they aren't here," I told her. "I'm not going to leave my baby girl's side. As long as I am here with her, I will make sure that we are both protected."

Sophia nodded. "Very well then. I never doubted your intelligence, my friend. My husband would not have stayed in business with you all of these years if you were not a smart man," she said. "I just wanted to make sure that your emotions are not getting the best of you. I understand how tough things have been recently. It's been an emotional time for us all. With Jada in the hospital, Cameron in prison, and Aaron gone ... I just wanted to check on you while I was here."

"I appreciate your concern, Sophia. I will be fine," I tried my best to assure her.

Sophia nodded, and we both turned back towards the window of Jada's hospital room. She continued to lay in the bed, motionless. She had been in the hospital since the night of the shooting – unconscious for most of that time due to the physical trauma her body had endured. While we both continued to look through the glass into Jada's room, Sophia spoke again.

"The baby is being released today. Daniella and I will be taking him to their house in Sandy Springs," she said. "You have my number if you need anything. I will be in touch."

I nodded in response. Sophia patted me on the shoulder before she started down the hallway leaving me alone with my thoughts.

I started to feel lightheaded and, in that moment, realized that I had not eaten all day. Glancing at my watch, I noticed that it was almost six o'clock in the evening. I pulled my cell phone from my pocket. I knew that Ayanna was on her way to the hospital so I would ask her to bring dinner.

But then I heard the alarm start to beep on one of the various machines in Jada's room. I looked over my shoulder for anyone who could help.

"Nurse!"

The word did not fully escape my lips before Jada's nurse and her team came rushing around the corner. Without looking at me directly, the nurse said, "Mr. Reid, please step aside."

I did as I was asked, allowing her into the room where she closed the door in my face.

I couldn't remember a time where I had ever felt so helpless in my life.

JADA

SIX MONTHS AFTER THE SHOOTING

*T*he room was still. With no movement from either of us, it was eerily quiet. In fact, the only sounds that could be heard were those that came from the steadily falling rain outside and the sound of the ticking clock on Dr. Sandra Peterson's wall. I ran my fingers through my curly mane and stared out of the floor to ceiling office windows. I swung my legs over the side of the large armchair and folded my arms across my chest. I sat in the office for almost forty minutes without saying a word. Only a few more minutes to go.

Sandra was a true professional. She did well to keep the frustration from her face, but I knew that she was bothered by our weekly silent sessions. She cleared her throat before speaking.

"Jada," her voice broke into my thoughts. "We've only got about fifteen minutes left. Would you like to talk today? It doesn't have to be about anything in particular. It's good if we could just get you to start talking and go from there."

I rolled my eyes and continued to look out the window.

"Yeah, I'm sure you don't want to sit here and discuss the lovely weather we're having."

"I'm open to discussing whatever you feel comfortable sharing. My goal is to start a conversation," Dr. Peterson said. "That's all I'm trying to accomplish today. You didn't say a word during your first four sessions. We're almost done with our session today, and still … not a word."

I turned my head to look at Sandra, but I didn't open my mouth to speak.

Dr. Peterson's face was full of sympathy, and I just wanted to roll my eyes again. I was so tired of everyone's pity. It almost made me sick to my stomach.

"Jada, your family is very concerned about you."

"Oh, is that why they've been forcing me to come here every week? I'm going to tell you like I've told them … I'm fine."

Sandra nodded in acknowledgment.

"I'm sure that you would like to believe that, but Jada … you have been through quite a bit in the past few years. Maybe it's starting to take a toll on you. When you complicate all that you've been through with the stress of being a new mother, it could be a lot for anyone to handle. There's nothing wrong with things affecting you more than you thought. Talking through your issues can be incredibly helpful for you, but first you have to be willing to acknowledge that the issues even exist."

I closed my eyes and let out a frustrated sigh. After a moment of silence passed between us, I swung my legs from the side of the armchair and turned around to face my doctor. "Fine, Sandra. Let's talk about it. Let's discuss whatever it's going to take for you to fix me. I would much rather spend my Tuesday afternoons doing something else."

Dr. Peterson leaned back in her seat with a pen in one hand a notepad in front of her, waiting for me to continue. I glanced outside at the steadily falling rain and let out an even deeper sigh while I shook my head. I turned back to face the doctor, and I finally began to speak.

"Honestly, I don't even know where you want me to start. I mean ... sure I've been under a lot of stress, but that just seems to be the story of my life. I've never dealt with loss well. I still struggle with my mother's death almost seven years later. Two people I grew up with were murdered – one I actually considered a friend who left behind a pregnant fiancé. My older brother was shot and killed. My longtime off and on boyfriend of ten years ended things for good and moved back to Texas. Two weeks after he left, I ended up miscarrying our child. It was our second miscarriage, and he ghosted me. He had nothing to say to me after finding out I was pregnant or after I lost the baby. His baby." I paused. "Fast forward to several months later, and I feel like I'm putting my life back together and things are falling into place. Then my younger brother ends up in federal prison facing charges that can put him away for life. It is stressful, and I am frustrated. At times, maybe I am a little overwhelmed. Bad things keep happening to my loved ones, and I feel like there isn't a damn thing I can do about it. Wouldn't that make you feel some type of way too?"

"Of course," Dr. Peterson responded. "Helplessness and hopelessness are terrible feelings to have. We can work on coping strategies to help you handle and process these situations."

The room fell quiet again, but we maintained eye contact for a few moments. Dr. Peterson cleared her throat and spoke again.

"But Jada ... if we are going to get to the bottom of everything then you have to be willing to talk about *everything*. You're going to have to discuss all the issues. It is vital that you acknowledge everything that has been triggering you."

"What do you mean?" I asked quickly.

Dr. Peterson hesitated briefly. "Jada, you need to talk about the night of the shooting. You haven't talked about your injuries, your son ... and you haven't mentioned Aaron at all."

I sat up straight in my chair.

"What about him?" I snapped.

"You're going to have to talk about it at some point. He's a large part of the reason you're sitting in front of me right now."

"My husband is dead. What in the world would make you think I would ever want to talk about that?"

"I've never been in your shoes so I can't pretend to sit here and say that I know how you feel, but what I do know is that denial will hinder the path to healing. My job is to help you. Let me help you, Jada."

I leaned back into my chair, closing my eyes. I wasn't trying to be difficult, but I didn't think that Dr. Peterson would understand that I didn't think I could ever be healed. Was it possible that someone could be so irretrievably broken to the point that they couldn't be made whole again? That was certainly how I felt. I didn't want to talk about Aaron, because I didn't think it would fix anything. I had to find a way to make Dr. Peterson understand that.

With my eyes still closed I asked, "Do you believe in soul mates?"

Sandra hesitated again but then answered, "Sure. Why not?"

I opened my eyes and looked directly into hers.

"For the longest time, I thought that Israel Mann was my soul mate – my one true love. I was convinced that he was going to eventually get his shit together, and we would have our happily ever. To be honest, I still had those thoughts in the back of my mind even when he showed up in town with another girlfriend. It has taken a great deal of hindsight for me to realize that he wasn't it. It took falling in love with Aaron Mercer for me to realize that I had been wrong about Israel all along. I believe that he loved me ... the best way he knew how anyway. I know that I loved him. I'm pretty sure that I always will in some capacity or another. However, love alone is not enough. I didn't have that understanding at the time, but I know that now."

Sandra nodded.

I continued to speak.

"My relationship with Israel was complicated ... convenient ... but it was also painful. I would be lying if I tried to say that it was all his fault. We both share the blame for that situation. We both hurt each other throughout the years, but I think that's the whole point of the matter. Real love ... true love is not supposed to hurt like that. Our love was immature. Although we grew up the relationship never did, and that's why it was never going to work. It took a while for me to come to grips with it, but I'm okay with it now."

The rain started to pour even harder, and I heard rumblings of thunder in the distance.

"My husband helped me realize what it's supposed to feel like when you are loving and being loved by the right person. We had our highs and lows. We had disagreements just like any other couple, but there is not a doubt in my mind that Aaron Mercer was created for me," I told my therapist. "Aaron provided everything that I never found with Israel. He made it his priority to protect our family and my heart. He loved me through the pain and the heartache of my past. He was patient with me and took the time to break down the walls that I had built. I discovered the best version of myself simply because of who he was and how he loved me."

I paused to take in another deep breath. Sandra continued to look at me, her eyes growing more sympathetic as I spoke. That was exactly what I didn't want. Her sympathy wasn't going to make me feel any better.

"So, try to imagine how I'm feeling right now," I stated. "Try for a minute to put yourself in my shoes. Imagine that after years of heartache and loss you finally find the love of your life. He proposes, you start to build a family or your own, and everything seems perfect. You feel complete after not even knowing that a part of you was missing. Then, unexpectedly you lose him. He loses his life trying to save yours, and now you're left to raise your son alone. No husband. No mother. No granny. One brother is dead, and the other one is locked up for God knows how long."

Glancing at the clock on the wall, I saw that our hour was drawing to a close. I started speaking like everyone wanted, but I didn't feel like it was going to help me.

"I feel like I'm in the worst imaginable hell on earth. I wake up every day in the house that we used to share haunted by memories of a life that will never be mine again. I am unable to escape him and unable to be with him at the same time. I still have family and friends, but it's not the same. My friend Nisha has been through a similar situation, but for the life of me I don't know how she has made it. Deep down I know that I have to keep going for my son, but I don't know how. I feel so lost and so incomplete and so lonely."

I stopped speaking and bit my lip. I dropped my head and stared at the ground while forcing my tears to stay put instead of spilling onto my cheeks. Crying wasn't going to make me feel better either. I had spent too many days and nights crying about the drama in my life.

After a brief moment, I looked back up at Dr. Peterson.

"Who even wants to wake up to a life like that every day?" I asked quietly.

JULIAN

"Man, who would have ever thought that we would be here?" PO asked, shaking his head in disbelief.

I shrugged my shoulders while we sat at the desk in my home office. PO's comment was real. Who would have ever thought that I would willingly be putting the game down? After thirty years of being the number one drug distributor in the metropolitan Atlanta area, I was preparing to turn over the reins and walk away from all that I had known for more than half of my life. I guess it could be said that all good things come to an end. I was just lucky that my end had come voluntarily and not due to death or incarceration. I was lucky for the partnership and friendship that I maintained with Manny Mercer throughout the years which allowed me to walk away so easily.

"I know. It still seems a little unbelievable," I said, "but the more I think about it, the more I know that this is the right thing for me to do at this time."

PO shifted in his chair. "How do you figure that?"

I took a sip of my drink before sitting it down on my desk. "Because I've had enough," I answered simply. "When I think about why I got in the game in the first place, it was to provide a better life for me and my family. Over the years I've built businesses, and I have more than enough money for myself and future generations. What I don't have is peace."

I paused to think about all that had transpired over the last few years. Losing my wife, mother, older son, and almost my younger daughter had certainly weighed heavily on me. I had climbed to some of the highest heights that my chosen profession allowed, but at what cost? Being involved in the drug game was no longer fulfilling. Being with my loved ones and ensuring their safety was what I truly desired.

"Yeah, I know it's been a rough couple of years for you and your fam, man. The streets won't be the same without you though. I truly hope you find the peace that you're looking for. You deserve it," PO said.

"I appreciate that. Speaking of people getting what they deserve ... it's time that you got what you deserve as well," I stated.

PO had a look of confusion on his face. "What do you mean?"

"I mean that Atlanta ... this whole organization that we've built ... it all belongs to you now. I'm turning the whole thing over to you," I answered. "No one else is more loyal or deserving of taking my place. You've earned it, PO. It's your time."

"Are you serious, man?"

I nodded. "As a heart attack," I responded. "By all accounts, you were instrumental in keeping things running with Aaron and Luke while I was away. Outside of Cameron and Deuce, you've been my right hand for years. You're more than capable."

"Thanks, man," PO said. He leaned forward and shook my hand. "If I'm capable, it's only from learning by your side. You've taught me everything that I know."

"Well, we've got a number of things to go over in the next couple of weeks. I've already spoken to Manny about the time needed for this transition. There are a few things we need to take care of in regard to business and money flow."

"I'm all ears."

"Manny doesn't want a bunch of new people coming into the fold. So, the deal is that you takeover with Zo by your side and let JB continue to run the muscle," I said.

PO nodded and responded, "No objections from me. JB's been doing a good job since we lost Blue, and Zo is more than ready."

"Good. I'm completely stepping away from the drug business, but I plan to keep my smaller family-owned businesses," I told him. "So, we need to work on getting other ventures set up for you to clean your money. I'm interested in hearing if you have any ideas, and I have Tony on standby to help with whatever you need."

"That all sounds good to me. I'm on board for whatever," PO said.

My ringing cell phone disturbed us. I looked down and knew I needed to answer the call once I saw the name on my caller ID.

"Excuse me. I really need to get this."

"No problem," PO said, standing up from his chair. "There's somewhere else I need to be anyway. I'll get up with you later."

PO quickly left the office, and I answered the call right before it went to voicemail.

"Hello."

I heard Dr. Sandra Peterson release a heavy sigh on the other end of the line. "Julian, I think we may have a problem."

"What's going on?" I asked with concern.

"You know I still feel pretty uncomfortable with all of this," she replied without answering my question. "This is against all types of rules and regulations. I could be in serious trouble if anyone found out what I was doing for you. I shouldn't be discussing anything she said to me."

"So, she actually started talking today?"

"She did. She sat there for almost forty-five minutes before she spoke, but eventually, she did speak … and Julian, that's the only reason why I'm calling you. What she said … I just … I'm genuinely concerned about her right now," Sandra responded. "She said something today that has me really concerned about her mental wellbeing."

I closed my eyes and pinched the bridge of my nose while I continued to hold the phone up to my ear. My concern for my younger daughter had been steadily growing over the last few months. In the six months since the night of the shooting, it was obvious to anyone who had been around Jada that she was struggling. It seemed like things had been on a steady decline for the last two years. Jada was having a hell of a time getting back on her feet and back to life as normal since she was released from the hospital. We were all concerned about her, and at my urging, she finally started to see Dr. Peterson a few weeks prior.

"What is your concern?" I asked.

"She made a comment that implied that waking up to her life isn't something she wants to do … Julian, I'm not convinced that she won't do something to hurt herself."

"Did she say anything else that made you think that she might harm herself in some way?"

"We didn't really have much time left after she made that statement. She talked about how everyday life was hard for her," Sandra responded. "I know you and Ayanna were concerned about her. That's why you had me work her into my schedule in the first place, but I think that this is more serious than either of you were expecting."

"What do I need to do?"

"Keep doing what you're doing, but make sure that there are eyes on her. Make sure that she continues to get help with the baby. Try to get her out of the house more and back to work full-time. She needs to keep herself busy, and she needs to have people around," Sandra answered. "Also, I wrote her a couple of prescriptions. You need to make sure that she gets them filled and actually takes them. Hopefully, I can get her to talk again next week. The more she speaks there's more of a chance I can make progress with her. I just wanted to let you know where we stand. This is very serious."

"I understand, and I appreciate the update. I'll stop by to see her today," I answered. "Let me know how next week goes."

"Of course. I'll talk to you later."

Sandra ended the call, and I took a sip from my drink before scrolling through my contacts. I located a number and placed another call which was answered quickly.

"Hey, Julian. What's going on, man? Is everything okay?"

"I don't know," I answered hesitantly. "How is everything coming along on your end?"

"Better than expected. I was actually planning to call you today," the person on the other end of the line said. "I should have everything wrapped up by Christmas."

"Good … good," I said. "The sooner the better. For everybody."

CAMERON

ime is relative or however the saying goes. I always wondered what that meant. A Google search explained it perfectly not too long ago. A brief summary of what I read states that time is not the same for every frame of reference. Two people in two different places can measure time at a different rate. I saw something else about different dimensions and what not, but I'm not going to get into all of that. That's not the point I'm trying to make. What I've come to understand is how the passage of time can feel so different for varying individuals. More specifically, I now understand how six months might not feel like a long time for some people, but it had felt like an eternity for me.

Life at the United States Federal Penitentiary in Atlanta was not as bad as I predicted, but it still missed having my freedom. There were enough people inside the prison walls that were affiliated with my father or the Mercers at one point or another so I never had to worry about my safety. The facility was old as shit though – well over a hundred years old, and it definitely showed. I would have given anything to be back home in my own bed without hundreds of men surrounding me on a daily basis. It was amazing how quickly I had gone from being on top of the world to being locked up in a Federal prison facing charges that put me at risk of never being a free man again.

If it wasn't bad enough that I was facing a mountain of time, I was stuck on the inside while so many changes were going on with my family. Rumor had it my father confirmed he was stepping away from the drug business. Although he was on my approved visitor list and had stopped by to see me more than anyone else, he never mentioned it to me directly. Not that I blamed him. He was doing the smart thing by keeping the microscope off of him as much as he could. It wasn't wise to openly discuss his business inside of prison walls. I can't say that I was surprised to hear about the recent development though. The possibility of my father retiring was kicked around since the moment he went to California to care for my ailing grandmother. What bothered me most was that he would be turning things over to PO since I was locked up. Without my older brother Deuce alive to assume the reins, the throne should have been mine.

Then there was my sister Jada.

The same night I was arrested, Mikey and Michaela Pitt – The Hit Twins – finally caught up to her. At thirty-eight weeks pregnant, she was shot twice at close range by Mikey Pitt. The stress of her injuries forced the medical professionals to deliver my nephew early. Luckily, the baby was fine, but Jada was in the hospital for a few weeks. To make matters worse, her husband, Aaron Mercer, ended up losing his life while trying to save hers. Although he and Luke were able to take out Mikey Pitt, Michaela fatally wounded Aaron before escaping the scene. I was glad that Jada and her son, Aaron Jr., were alive, but she was having a tough time trying to get back to normal.

Six months definitely felt like an eternity to me. It didn't help that I dealt with a huge amount of regret. I was indicted on a number of charges including federal drug trafficking, conspiracy, and murder. Through the grand jury process, my legal team discovered that my ex-girlfriend, Shannon, was working with Drug Enforcement Agency agent Kendra Franklin, the woman I had formed a romantic relationship with and knew as Brianna Taylor. Together, the two knew things that I never should have told anyone who wasn't working with my father's business. I had no other choice but to trust the legal team my father and Manny Mercer put together. However, I knew that Shannon and Agent Franklin knew things that could put me away forever. What ate away at me was the fact that it could have all been avoided. Had I not cheated on Shannon, Kendra Franklin would not know incriminating information about me, and Shannon would not be so pissed that she actually decided to cooperate with the Feds.

I shook my head while I laid on the bed in my cell.

I sure knew how to pick them.

My attorneys were actively working to delay my trial because we needed time. With the overwhelming closing rate of the Federal prosecutors not appearing in my favor, I knew that we needed more time for my father and Manny Mercer to come up with a plan. A guilty verdict would not reflect well on my dad, the Cartel, or anyone who did business with us. There was already fallout from the dealers on my dad's team that were not pleased with the heat a federal investigation was putting on our organization. We needed to find a way to end the mayhem and put this all behind us. The sooner we could do that the better things would be for me, but until then I had nothing but time on my hands.

LUKE

"I still don't understand why you had to go to Atlanta the morning after Thanksgiving but okay," Nakia said with a slight attitude. I placed her call on speakerphone and started the rental car. "I thought you were done with Atlanta, but you flew up there for one conversation. That's weird."

I shook my head and laughed while I pulled the vehicle out of the airport rental company parking lot and started towards the main interstate.

"Baby, we're never going to be done with Atlanta. It's one of our most profitable markets," I explained. "Eventually I won't really have to come up here anymore, but we're working through a transition right now. There's a pretty important conversation that I need to have, but I promise I'll be back home tonight."

"Yeah, okay. In the meantime, I'm going to take this money you left and go Black Friday shopping."

I laughed and said, "I have no doubt about that. Enjoy yourself."

"I absolutely will. I may even get something nice for you … with your own money," she laughed. "Anyway, be safe, baby. I'll see you later tonight. I love you."

"I love you too."

I ended the call and continued towards my destination. Before long I pulled into Julian Reid's neighborhood and made my way to the back of the neighborhood where Julian's house sat in a quiet cul-de-sac. Pulling into the driveway, I parked next to PO's vehicle before exiting the car and jogging up the steps to the front door. I hated the cold Atlanta winter weather. I couldn't wait to get back home. I rang the doorbell and was soon greeted by Julian's housekeeper, Yolanda. When she came to the door, she had a giggling baby boy on her hip. From the wild curly hair and dimples, I already knew that it was Jada and Aaron's son, Aaron Jr. He had changed a lot since the last time I saw him, but he looked so much like his father.

"Mr. Malone, come inside," Yolanda welcomed me with a warm smile. "They are waiting for you in the office. Follow me."

I followed Yolanda up the stairs to Julian's home office. AJ smiled at me while he played with the baby toy he held in his hands. He looked so much like Aaron it was mind-blowing. I sighed at the thought of what Jada dealt with the past several months. It couldn't have been easy for her to see Aaron's face every single time she looked at their son. Yolanda led me into the room where I was greeted by both; meanwhile, she excused herself, taking little AJ along with her. I shook hands with both Julian and PO before sitting down in my seat.

"You watching AJ today?" I asked Julian.

He nodded. "Jada's down at the boutique for their Black Friday sale so I figured I would spend some time with my grandson," he answered. "They were over yesterday for Thanksgiving, and AJ stayed the night. Jada should be back later this evening to pick him up."

"Damn. I'm sorry that I'm going to miss her. I've been trying to reach her for a couple of weeks, but she hasn't been answering her phone," I stated. "How is she doing?"

Julian hesitated and shrugged his shoulders. "Some days are better than others. I'll let her know that you asked about her. I'm sure she will appreciate it."

After a few more moments of small talk, we got down to business.

"Any word on Michaela Pitt?" Julian asked.

He and PO both looked at me expectantly. Unfortunately, I had to shake my head in response.

"Nah, man. I wish I had an update, but I don't. I don't know anything new from the last update two weeks ago," I answered. "Hopefully she'll be taken care of by Christmas."

"I hope so," Julian responded. "But let me bring you up to speed on what PO and I have been working on in regard to the transition."

I sat back and listened for the next several minutes while Julian and PO brought me up to speed. They working to properly sever Julian's business ties from the organization, and

Julian's son in law, Tony, was working alongside them to secure new businesses for PO. They already met with the majority of their distributors to inform them of the changes and how business would be conducted moving forward. If things continued according to plan, PO would be fully functioning as the head of the Atlanta market by the beginning of the New Year. Manny would be pleased to hear of the progress.

"So, what issues are you facing since word spread about the change in leadership?" I questioned.

PO sat up a little straighter in his chair. "I wouldn't necessarily call them issues, but a few members of the crew have raised a couple of concerns," he responded. "Questions have been asked about Cameron's pending trial and what impact it may have on the business. A few have asked if it is really the right time to switch things up."

"I've assured them that now is the perfect time," Julian spoke up. "With Cameron in the spotlight, I should probably lay low anyway. On top of my personal reasons for stepping away, it's probably best for the business if the Reid name is no longer associated."

I nodded in agreement with Julian's comment. To PO I said, "Julian's right. Now is the perfect time, and he's stepping away to take care of his family. Jada needs help. Cameron needs help. That's where his focus should be."

"I completely understand that," PO said.

"Besides," I said in a joking tone, "If anyone else wants to question our moves, let them know that they can speak with Manny Mercer about that. I bet that will shut them up real fast."

PO laughed. "Hell yeah."

"Now about Cameron ..." I let my voice trail off.

I came to Atlanta to discuss the progress with the transition plans. Manny was in the midst of a round of chemotherapy and not up for traveling. However, I had a message for PO and Julian.

"What about him?" Julian asked.

"I spoke to Manny about the options. There are three ways that you can move forward, and it's ultimately for the two of you to decide," I told them. "First option is that the Cartel gets involved and makes some moves that would ensure the case gets dropped, and Cameron returns home a free man. It will be risky, but I'm confident we would pull it off."

"Sounds good to me. What's the downside of that plan?" PO asked.

"If we do that, Cameron returns home, but he's no longer associated with the business."

"What are the other two options?" Julian questioned.

"Second option is that we still make the necessary moves for him to come home, but if you're dead set on having him involved in the business you would be doing so without the support of Manny Mercer. PO, you would need to find a new connect."

PO shook his head while he quietly settled into his chair. Finding a new supplier was the last thing he would want to do after immediately assuming Julian's position. I continued to speak.

"The last option is that Manny and I do nothing. Cameron stays in jail and potentially has to eat those charges if his lawyer can't find a way to get him off," I explained. "The Atlanta organization moves forward with Manny as your supplier while you rebrand and distance yourself from the Reid family."

Julian and PO sat quietly while they contemplated my words. I don't think either man was blindsided by the options before them. They were both business-minded individuals that were very familiar with the way that Manny Mercer conducted business. Unfortunately, Cameron was reckless enough to put them in their current position, and I knew it would be a tough decision for them to make.

"I understand if you need time to discuss your options," I

stated, "but I would encourage you to come to a decision before the beginning of the year. We would like to know the plan before PO completely takes over."

Julian nodded. "Fair enough."

"Well gentlemen, it's been a pleasure catching up with you both, but I have another stop to make before I head back to the airport," I said, standing up from my seat. I shook their hands again. "PO, congrats man. You definitely deserve it."

PO nodded. "Thanks, man."

"Julian, can you ask Jada to call me?" I asked. "I know she's going through a lot. I don't want to be a bother, but Aaron and I were raised like brothers. I know he would want me to check on her and the baby."

Julian nodded. "Of course. I'll relay the message when she stops by," he said. "Tell Manny that I hope to have a decision for him sooner rather than later. Cam's already been in there six months. I know he's itching to get home."

"Will do," I said, turning to exit the room.

JADA

"*S*o, what do you think about this dress, Ms. Mercer?" the bridal consultant asked. "Do you like this one?"

I looked at my reflection in the full-length mirror with a blank stare. I honestly didn't know how I felt as I stared at my body in the off the shoulder, floor length chiffon magenta gown. After three and a half years of being engaged, Vanessa and DJ finally set a wedding date. As her maid of honor, I joined Vanessa and her bridesmaids to look for our dresses. I turned to get a side view in the mirror, but I was not sure how to answer the sales consultant's question.

My appearance had definitely changed since the birth of my son. Several months later I was still trying to get comfortable with my new body. Without the energy or the motivation to hit the gym, everything was fuller – my face, my breasts, my thighs. Although those closest to me insisted I looked fine, I was not so convinced. Standing in front of the mirror in the sweetheart neckline dress, staring at my bubbling cleavage, I felt severely uncomfortable. I shook my head.

"I don't think I like this one either," I finally answered.

"No problem," the bridal consultant quickly said with a smile on her face. She had been so helpful. I felt sorry that I was such a difficult customer. "Why don't you go on and change out of that one. I'll pull a few more styles."

I thanked her and she disappeared onto the sales floor. Vanessa approached me before I could step back into the fitting room.

"Hey ... is everything alright?" Vanessa asked. There was a hint of concern in her voice, but the smile on her face was carefree.

I couldn't identify with the feeling of being carefree. I marveled at how Vanessa's life had always been so easy and carefree. The only child of two successful corporate attorneys, she came from old money on both sides. While I completed my studies at Clark Atlanta University, Vanessa graduated from Spelman. Although she was the proud owner of a degree in Political Science, Vanessa had no plans to actually use her degree. Other than occasional modeling, she had never worked a day in her life. She did not have to. She was a trust fund baby with a famous, wealthy fiancé. Her bank accounts were doing just fine.

"Yeah, I'm fine. Why are you asking me that?" I asked.

"It's just ... that's probably the fifth dress you've tried on, and you haven't liked any of them. You've been on the phone half the time we've been here. It just seems like you're a little distracted and physically here but not really *here*," she responded. "Nisha and the other bridesmaids have already selected their dresses. I just thought–"

Vanessa stopped speaking when my cell phone started to ring again. I stepped into the fitting room to check the caller ID. Vanessa rolled her eyes.

"I need to get this."

I answered the call and spoke with Mia, the manager at Carmen's, about an employee issue before ending the call and turning back towards Vanessa, who had her hands on her hips.

"What?" I asked defensively.

"Jada, I understand you have a lot going on, but I only asked for an hour or two of your time today," she said with a disappointed look on her face. "It's taken weeks to find a day that worked with your schedule, and I still only have half your attention. This isn't what I expected when I asked you to be my maid of honor. I feel like I've had to chase you down for help."

Vanessa was right. She asked me two months prior if I was up for the task of being her maid of honor. At the time I agreed, but it was obvious I had dropped the ball. I wasn't there for her like either of us thought I would be. I tried to get back into the groove of things with work, but there were still days when I stayed in the house with AJ, not wanting to do anything. Vanessa wasn't the only person I had let down. With people expecting more from me than I currently had to give, I felt like I had been disappointing people left and right. I needed to find a way to be there for my friend – the friend who had always been there for me.

"I'm sorry, Ness. I just –"

"Forget it," Vanessa sighed, cutting me off. "I know you need to get back home to AJ. I'll just tell the consultant to hold off on the other dresses. You can come back another day when you actually have time to do this … whenever that may be."

"Vanessa, wait!"

"No. If you can't pull it together to be here for me, you never should have said yes."

Vanessa walked off in search of the bridal consultant before I could say anything else. I hesitated before closing the door to the fitting room and changing back into my clothes. When I stepped out of the fitting room everyone was gone except for Nisha.

"Where's Vanessa?"

"She said she had to leave, but that she'll call you later."

I sighed and called over Danny, one of the bodyguards that

replaced Harold and Vic. After the shooting at my condo, they were both fired. My father and the Mercers put together a brand-new security team, and Danny was the person with me the most. I had no choice but to get used to having someone around at all times. We started the walk towards the parking lot where our vehicles were parked next to each other. I paused when I reached the rear passenger door of the Escalade. Danny opened my door before climbing into the driver's seat. I turned towards Nisha.

"I'm trying Nisha, but I just feel like such a shitty friend right now," I said. "It's almost been seven months. I'm really trying to put my best foot forward, but sometimes it's just too hard. How did you do it? How did you get back to normal after Kelvin died?"

Nisha looked at me with sympathetic eyes. "I know you're trying, Jada. To be honest, it's almost been two years since Kel passed, and I'm still not back to normal. You'll eventually get to a better place mentally and emotionally, but it's going to take some time," she said. "Everybody knows that. Vanessa does too. She just has a lot going on with the wedding, especially the closer that we get to the date. Don't beat yourself up about anything she said to you in there. You're doing fine, sweetie."

I nodded and hugged my friend. "Thanks, girl. Let me go on and get out of here.."

Danny started the short drive back to my house. Ayanna agreed to watch AJ while I went dress shopping. When Danny pulled into the driveway of my house a frown spread across my face when I noticed Julissa's car parked in front. Julissa was Aaron's housekeeper who never particularly cared for me. Since Aaron had been gone, I had not called on her for assistance. I entered the house in search of my sister who I found in the nursery.

"Yanni, what the hell?"

Ayanna held a finger up to her lips before removing the

sleeping AJ from her shoulder and placing him into his crib. She turned the baby monitor on and headed out to the hallway with me right on her heels.

"What's going on?"

"AJ just had a bottle and fell asleep about fifteen minutes ago," she answered, looking at her watch.

"Not that. What is Julissa doing here?"

"I gave her a call," Ayanna answered nonchalantly. "The house was a mess when I got here, Jada. She brought some groceries, and she's helping to clean up around here. She scheduled for the old cleaning crew to come early in the week."

I let out a deep breath before responding. I had no idea why I was so bothered by Ayanna's statement and Julissa's presence, but I was.

"Did you just call my house filthy?" I asked with an attitude.

Ayanna sighed. "Jada, that's not what I meant, but I do feel like Julissa could help," she said. "There's nothing wrong with a little assistance every now and then. I know you're trying to get back into the swing of things, but you're still a working, single mother. This house is huge. No one can maintain a place this big by themselves. Let Julissa and the cleaners help. That's what they're getting paid to do."

"With what money?" I snapped.

"Aaron had his affairs in order, Jada, and we've had this conversation before. Tony and your accountant keep you well informed. The life insurance policies and accounts he left behind ensure that you'll never have to worry about money. I don't know why you're so reluctant to spend the money that was intended to take care of you."

"Because it's unnecessary," I said. "I understand that you are just trying to help, but I'm going to tell you exactly what I have told everybody else ... I am fine."

Ayanna stared at me silently. She contemplated if she should say the words on the tip of her tongue. After a few quiet seconds, she did.

"Are you really fine, Jada?" she asked. "Your emotions have been all over the place. You still lock yourself up in this house for days at a time. You haven't been sleeping or eating properly. You finally started going to the therapist, but you won't take any of the meds she prescribed. Sometimes you can barely get yourself out of the bed. I am concerned about the way you've been caring for yourself and AJ."

"AJ is fine."

"I know he is. You have a healthy happy boy despite the way that he was brought into this world. He needs a healthy, happy mama," Ayanna stated. "I know you want to give him that, but you're not there yet."

"Are you calling me a bad mother?"

"No. Of course not," Ayanna said, shaking her head. "What I'm trying to say is that we need to find a way to get back to normal. I understand everything that has happened, but Jada … you've been a zombie on autopilot for months."

She was right. I had been out of it.

Ayanna rubbed my shoulder and pulled me into a hug. "It's going to be okay, Jada. I promise. Everybody wants what's best for you and AJ. Just let us help you."

Hours after Ayanna left my house, I laid in my bed with AJ beside me. He played with his toys while looking at cartoons on my tablet. I was exhausted, and I hoped that AJ tired himself soon, so that we could both get a decent night of rest. I reached for my cell phone and scrolled through a few emails. My eyes rested on an email from Dr. Sandra Peterson's office asking me to confirm our appointment for the upcoming week. I hesitated.

I initially put up a fight when my father urged me to seek professional help for the stress and depression I faced. I don't know why I had been so resistant. I was starting to realize that maybe everyone was right. I was having trouble getting back to who I was before the shooting. Maybe it was time I listened to the professional and followed her advice.

I opened the email and responded to let Dr. Peterson's office, letting them know that I would see them Tuesday.

JULIAN

I sat in the designated visitor's area waiting for Cameron to be escorted out. A week had passed since PO and I met with Luke. I took some time on my own to come to a decision. After speaking with PO, it appeared that we were on the same page. I needed to speak with Cameron to plant the seed in his mind that things would be drastically different if and when we were able to get him released from prison.

I looked around the visitation room at the other families meeting with loved ones. I spent so much time and energy trying to prevent my family from ever being in this situation. Somewhere along the way, I made a misstep with Cameron. Somehow, I failed him. It was my job to provide the proper guidance to my children to make sure that they avoided situations like the one Cameron was facing. While contemplating the options from Manny Mercer, I knew that there was no available choice that would make everyone happy. With that being the case, PO and I ultimately had to do what was best for the business and the majority of the team – regardless of how Cameron would feel about it. With my departure from the business, change was on the horizon for everyone. Cameron would be no different.

A few minutes later, Cameron was led into the room and seated across from me.

"Pops, what's good?"

I shrugged my shoulders. "Same shit just a different day."

"How's everybody doing?"

"Everybody's fine. Ayanna and Tony are doing pretty well.

Katy is doing great well in school. Ayanna mentioned that she and Tony may try again for another child soon."

"Oh yeah. That's what's up. How's Jada?"

I sighed heavily. She was starting to be receptive to therapy but otherwise, her progress was slow. I didn't want to lie to Cameron, but I didn't think that it would do him any good to worry about his sister while he was stuck behind bars.

"She's coming along. You know Christmas is her favorite holiday, and it's right around the corner. Hopefully that will put her in better spirits. AJ is doing pretty well. He's got two teeth at the bottom, and he's crawling all over the place."

Cameron nodded and a smile spread across his face. "That's what's up. What else is going on?"

"That's actually why I came by today. I wanted to give you an update on something. You know that there are changes going on in connection with … my retirement," I said in a lower tone of voice.

Cameron leaned a little closer to me. I knew that I needed to choose my words carefully inside the walls of the prison.

"Changes are being made to the business. You already know that PO will be in charge going forward. There's something else I need to let you know so you're not blindsided when you come home."

A look of uneasiness appeared on Cameron's face.

"What change?"

"No one with the last name Reid will be working with the business. That includes you."

Cameron's face wrinkled into a frown.

"What do you mean?"

I cleared my throat. "I mean what I said. Look … I know that's probably not what you want to hear, but it's necessary. It's the only way you're going to come home."

"Oh yeah?"

Cameron shook his head and sat straight up, pulling away from me.

"Who made that call?"

I shrugged my shoulders. Cameron wasn't a complete idiot. He already knew the answer to that question, but I decided to respond anyway. "Who do you think, Cam? Again, I know this isn't a decision that you're happy about, but it's best for all parties involved."

"Yeah okay. You mean it's what's best for the Mer –"

I raised my hand to silence him. He knew better than to mention the Mercer name.

"You'll be coming home to a stress-free environment, and you know money isn't an issue. We still have our family-run businesses and there's plenty of money saved. I'll figure out something for you to do. You're going to be just fine."

"I suppose I don't have a choice."

"No. You don't."

For the remainder of our visit, Cameron and I made small talk. Although he didn't raise the issue again, I knew he was bothered with the decision that had been made. However, he was right. He didn't have a choice. When he had the freedom and authority to make decisions, he chose poorly. When I reached my car, I pulled my phone from my pocket and placed a call while I sat behind my steering wheel.

"Julian, what's up?" Luke greeted. "How's everything going?"

"Pretty well. No complaints. I just wanted to let you know that PO and I have come to a decision."

"Is that so?"

"Yeah, and I just spoke to Cameron and gave him a heads up. Moving forward you won't have to worry about him being involved with the business. PO and I are on the same page. Cameron has no choice but to accept it. It's the best thing for everyone involved, and he needs to come home. I don't think he's prepared to spend the rest of his life in prison."

"I agree," Luke said. "I figured that would be the best move. I just wanted you and PO to come to that agreement by yourselves. I'll let the boss know. Give us a little time to work out the details before we take action. Like I already said, it will be a little risky, but we're going to hold up our end of the bargain and get your son home."

"I have no doubt," I told him. Changing the subject, I asked, "Did you ever hear from Jada?"

"Yeah. I spoke to her earlier this week. She sounded better than the last time we spoke, and she's planning to come down here soon to spend some time with Olivia and the family. I'll see her then."

"Sounds good. Just keep me updated on the plan as it progresses. PO and I are still moving forward with the transition. Everything should be handled by the first of the year."

"Perfect. I'll let you know when we're ready to make a move. We'll get Cameron home as soon as we can."

PO

*P*ulling the blunt away from my lips, I exhaled deeply as I continued to steer my car towards my destination. With Christmas just a few days away and the New Year rapidly approaching, there were only a few days remaining before I assumed complete control of the Atlanta organization. Being handed the reins to Julian Reid's empire had come as a bit of a surprise. Only because I wasn't sure I would ever see the day he retired. I had started working for Julian when I was seventeen years old. Twenty-five years later, there was no doubt that I had paid my dues. I was working with Julian when Cameron was still in diapers. Without Deuce alive to see the day his old man gave up the game, it made sense that I would be next in line.

That's why I incorrectly assumed the transition would go over smoothly. Although we weren't having issues like the ones we faced battling KS9 or the Pitt twins, things still weren't going as smoothly as I would have liked. On one hand, I couldn't fault the guys for the concerns they had. With Cameron facing federal charges for crimes associated with the organization, it was only natural to wonder if the rest of us were under a microscope as well. One of my first orders of business was to ensure that Mayor Richardson and local law enforcement were back on our side. Although Julian never steered me wrong, the powers that be felt that he dropped the ball – leading them to withdraw their support and protection. I could not afford that going forward. If I was going to lead the Atlanta division of the Ramirez Cartel back to greatness, I needed to have a strong team – a team that included the mayor and chief of police. They were essential to Julian's success for many years, and I planned for them to be essential to mine as well.

I also needed to make sure that I maintained the status quo with our dealers. Besides the change in leadership, nothing else major needed to change for them. Nothing changed with our product. Nothing changed with our traps. I didn't even plan to change anything with our processes – for the time being. Business would continue to function as usual except for the fact that everyone would report to me instead of the man who had been in charge for the last thirty years.

I pulled into the parking lot of the 24-hour wash and fold that Tony helped me secure. It was one of the many businesses purchased in order to assist with the laundering of our dirty money. After shutting off my engine, I entered the business, greeting a few of the customers and employees on the way to a back office. Using my key, I unlocked the door to the large office where Zo and JB were already waiting.

"What's up?" I greeted both men.

"Shit's good for the most part. Another busy week in the books," JB said.

"For the most part?" I asked. "What's the problem?"

Zo sighed and shrugged his shoulders. "We had a little bit of a problem collecting some of the money."

"Some of the money? You know that ain't no type of shit I'm trying to hear right now."

"It's really just the money from Prime," Zo explained. "He didn't show up to the drop off, and we haven't been able to get in touch with him."

Prime was one of the newer members of the crew. We rarely added to the team unless there was a crucial need. Cameron Reid was a perfect example of what could happen if you trusted too many of the wrong people. Prime joined the team because of a crucial need. After Ryan switched sides by joining Caleb Bridges and KS9, one of our more profitable territories was without a leader. Prime stepped up and took over that location for us. Since taking over, he reclaimed a stronghold in the area by bringing in more of a profit than we had seen from that location in close to two years. However, he did not like to follow the same rules and processes that the other dealers abided by. Prime was increasingly becoming more of a pain in my side, and I had not even officially taken over yet. I needed to set the example that no one dealer was above any other. If there were rules to be followed, they would apply to all involved in the organization, regardless of how much money any one player was bringing into the fold.

"Did you go by his spot?"

"We rolled by the trap. He wasn't there?" JB answered.

"Did you go by his house?"

"I was waiting on you, boss."

"Alright then. Let's ride," I told them both. "I don't have time for niggas to challenge the system, and I want my damn money. We ain't never accepted excuses for missing a money drop before. We're not about to start now."

JB and Zo hopped up from their seats and followed me without question. We climbed into my truck and started towards Prime's house. When I reached our destination, I shook my head at the sight before me. Several cars were parked along the street on both sides while loud music could be heard outside of the residence. He had time to throw a party at his crib, but not enough time to drop off the money. That was completely unacceptable. I put the car in park and started towards the front door with JB and Zo on my heels. I guess since I was always the silent type people thought it was okay to challenge me.

Prime was about to learn otherwise.

With the front door unlocked, we walked right into the house. The house was packed with people smoking, drinking, and partying. I shook my head and exhaled heavily. If I didn't get my money, I was about to ruin everyone's night. After a little searching, I found Prime seated in a corner of his dining room. He had a bottle of Hennessy in front of him and an attractive female in his lap. JB and Zo followed while I walked right up to him.

Prime stopped laughing when he saw me, but he maintained the smile on his face. "Boss man, what brings you by this evening? I'm surprised to see you."

"Yeah kind of like how I'm surprised I had to come here," I told him. "We need to speak outside."

"Oh yeah? I'm kind of in the middle of something right now."

JB took a step towards Prime, his hand resting on the gun he had in his waistband. "Aye, my man … the boss said he needs to speak to you outside. I suggest you get your ass up and go outside."

Prime smirked at JB before cutting his eyes towards me. He hesitated for a brief moment before asking the young woman in his lap to excuse herself and followed us into his front yard. I stopped walking a few yards away from my truck.

"Alright, boss. What's all the drama about?"

"Ain't no drama. You know one of the only things I care about is money. You didn't show up to the money drop and you didn't answer your phone when my men tried to reach you. I want my money, man."

"My bad, PO. I got a little tied up celebrating my boy's birthday. I'll get it to you tomorrow."

I shook my head, and Zo spoke up.

"Wrong answer, bruh. You'll get the money now."

Prime shook his head and laughed. "In the middle of a party? You want me to walk through a packed house with that type of cash? I don't need niggas knowing where I keep my funds or how much I have on hand. That doesn't make any type of sense."

"It don't make any sense that you would have the money here in the first place."

The friendly smile dropped from Prime's face and he took a few steps in my direction. "Look, man –"

As soon as he was close enough, I grabbed him by his shirt, interrupting whatever point he thought he was trying to make. "I don't give a fuck about whatever bullshit is about to come out of your mouth. We're doing way too much talking anyway. JB and Zo can go in the house with you, get the money, and come out the back. I don't give a fuck, but I know I better have that goddamn money in the next five minutes."

Prime snatched away from me with his face twisted in anger. "Alright man, damn!" He turned towards JB and Zo. "Come the fuck on."

They followed him back into the house and the ongoing party. A few minutes later, JB and Zo came out the back of the house with a couple of duffle bags in town and met me at my truck. I shook my head while they climbed into my ride. I started back towards the laundromat, and Zo sat quietly in the passenger seat for a few minutes before turning towards me.

"Aye, PO, I don't really like how that nigga Prime moves, man."

"What do you mean?"

"Julian hasn't even completely sat it down yet, and he's already out here fucking up. The nigga's a loose cannon. It's just something about him that doesn't sit right with me."

I nodded. "I feel that same way and trust me. He will be monitored closely. I don't have time for any extra bullshit right now. I'm focused on making sure things keep rolling smoothly and getting the mayor and PD back on our side."

Zo nodded and turned back towards the window. Taking over for Julian meant that I was going to have my hands full with several things that were much more important than chasing down a dealer for my money. If Prime didn't get with the program soon, I would have to make an example out of him for everyone to see.

JULIAN

Standing in my kitchen, I placed a few ice cubes in a glass and then covered the ice with cognac. I took a sip of my drink while listening to the sounds of my family members gathered in the great room. It was Christmas evening and like normal, we were together to celebrate the holiday. Ayanna was the only one of my children present, but plenty of extended family had come over and we were having a good time in each other's presence. After a few more sips of my drink, I was preparing to rejoin my family when I heard the front door open.

"Auntie Jay!" I heard Katy's voice followed by the sound of her running footsteps.

Jada had finally shown up.

I looked down at my watch and shook my head. It was a little after six o'clock. She was supposedly *"on the way"* for hours. I let out a deep sigh before heading into the foyer. Jada had AJ in one arm and the diaper bag and purse on her other arm while she spoke with Ayanna and Tony.

"I'm glad you made it," Ayanna said, taking Jada's purse and diaper bag. "I tried to call you a few times. I wasn't sure we would see you today."

Jada shrugged her shoulders. She looked extremely tired.

"I told Dad I was coming. I just had to finish packing, but I'm here now," she said. "There are some gifts in my truck. Tony, do you mind?"

"Of course not," Tony said.

He slipped into his coat and headed out to Jada's car.

"Packing?" Ayanna asked.

Jada turned her attention towards me.

"Hey, daddy," she greeted me with a hug as I joined them.

"Hey, baby girl."

"What were you packing for?" Ayanna asked.

"I'm going to Miami in the morning. It's AJ's first holiday season, and Sophia and Olivia are anxious to spend time with him," Jada answered. "Besides, maybe a little sun will do me good."

"It couldn't hurt," I responded, taking AJ from her arms. "Come on in and sit down."

We headed into the living room joining my sister Jackie, her husband and sons, my sister Vita, and a host of other family members. Tony brought Jada's gifts into the house and helped her pass them out. After we finished our gift exchange, I headed back into the kitchen to refill my glass. Jada joined me a few moments later.

"What do you have to drink?" she asked.

"Drink?"

"Yeah. Wine? Bourbon?"

I looked at her with concern in my eyes. "Are you supposed to be drinking right now?" I asked. "I thought Dr. Peterson said –"

Jada waved me off.

"That's not an issue."

"What do you mean it's not an issue?"

Jada hesitated. "I'm not taking those pills," she answered. I opened my mouth to speak but she raised her hand to stop me. "Before you get all worked up … I tried them, and I didn't feel like myself. I felt even worse. I'm trying to get back to normal …

whatever that's going to look like now. I don't want to be dependent on meds to make it through the day. I'm fine, Dad. I promise. I'm doing a lot better than I was a few weeks ago, even though I may not look like it."

"You look great, Jada. Beautiful as always," I told her. "I just want to make sure you're taking care of yourself."

"I am."

I took a sip of my drink instead of responding. Jada made her way around the kitchen, pulling down a glass from the cabinet and filling it with a white wine before returning to the great room with the rest of the family. I was making a mental note to speak with Dr. Peterson when my cell phone rang. Recognizing the number on the screen, I answered the call quickly.

"Hello."

"Julian, Merry Christmas!" the voice on the other end of the line greeted with excitement.

"Merry Christmas to you as well."

"I have some good news for you. Probably the best present you're going to receive all day."

"What is that?"

"Michaela Pitt is dead."

"For real?"

"For real."

I released a deep sigh of relief. I was holding onto much angst and anxiety over the fact that Michaela Pitt was still walking this earth after what she had done to my daughter and her husband. Finally, I would be able to sleep a little easier at night knowing that at least one threat facing my family was finally removed for good.

"You're right. That's the best present I've received all day," I said, turning to look towards my family room. "I'm sure Jada will be excited to hear the news as well."

"Let me tell her."

My forehead wrinkled into a deep frown.

"What?" I questioned.

"I know she's coming to Miami in the morning. I think I should be the one to deliver the good news."

I released another sigh. "I'm not so sure about that. She's really been dealing with a lot. She's been struggling ever since —"

"Julian, there's a lot that needs to be cleaned up. Let me be the one to handle this."

I hesitated once more.

"Fine," I reluctantly agreed.

After a few more moments of conversation, we ended our call. I rejoined my family members in the great room, savoring the joyous moments of togetherness. It was refreshing to see Jada among her loved ones with a rare smile on her face. Although I knew Jada would find relief in knowing that Michaela Pitt was dead, I was a little uncomfortable with the fact that she had no idea what she would be walking into when she arrived in Miami.

JADA

*I*t took me forever to get out of the bed on Christmas day and make it over to my father's house, but I was glad that I eventually showed up. I enjoyed myself so much that I ended up staying way longer than I intended. Getting in the bed later than planned made for a groggy morning, and I struggled to make sure that AJ and I made it to the airport on time. I could not wait to get to the Mercer estate and climb into bed for a long nap.

My eyes were closed, and I rested against the headrest. Since I was still unable to go most places without security, Danny had accompanied us on our trip. Julio picked us up from the airport and drove towards the Mercers' residence with Danny in the passenger seat. AJ and I sat comfortably in the middle row of the Escalade. The previous day I told my father that I was doing fine, and for the most part that was true. However, I was so inexplicably tired. I just felt like there was no such thing as getting enough sleep. After a brief FaceTime call with Olivia and Sophia to let them know we were on the way, I closed my eyes for a brief rest.

There were literally not enough words to describe how tired

I truly was. I was relieved when Sophia called asking to keep AJ for a few days. I told my family that I would be staying in Miami, but I had really planned to drop AJ off and return home so I could catch up on sleep and work. For the last several months I tried to balance life as a widow, single mother, entrepreneur, daughter, sister, and friend. I was drained. While Julio continued our drive, I dozed off at some point. I was startled from my impromptu nap when AJ squealed and threw his toy onto my lap. My eyes slowly opened. I grabbed the toy and placed it back into his chubby little hands. I smiled at him and ran my fingers through his wild, curly hair. He gazed at me with a wide grin, displaying two teeth at the bottom and a set of dimples identical to his father's. A surge of emotion washed over me. The smallest things could trigger my grief. It came and went in waves.

I turned away from AJ opting to look out of the window while Julio approached the security gate leading onto the estate. He guided the vehicle past security up to the front of the house, stopping in the circular driveway right at the main entrance. Danny exited the passenger seat and opened my door. I stepped out of the vehicle, turning my back towards the house to unbuckle AJ's car seat. I heard the front door open and close and the clicking of Sophia's heels as she approached me. I glanced over my shoulder and smiled at her. I don't think a day had ever existed where Sophia Mercer was not the picture of perfection. I pulled AJ into my arms right as Sophia reached my side.

"Mija, how are you?" she asked, kissing me on the cheek. "How was your flight?"

"It was smooth. Thank you."

Sophia smiled as she took AJ from my arms. "Mi hermoso nieto," she said, kissing his full cheeks.

I shouldered AJ's diaper bag and smiled at the interaction between my mother in law and my son. Even in Aaron's absence, Sophia was a very involved grandmother. It warmed my heart to witness the bond they were building. Sophia was instructing Julio and Danny to grab the rest of the bags when I heard the door open again. I figured it would be Olivia racing out to greet us. Sophia quickly and firmly grabbed my arm, stopping me from looking towards the entrance of the house.

There was a nervous look on her face that caused my eyebrows to furrow and an uneasiness in my stomach.

"Jada, there is something you must know," Sophia nervously said.

"Ma, I got it."

My heart skipped a beat when I heard the familiar voice. I thought I was hallucinating. Outside of my dreams, it was a voice I had not heard in seven months. I quickly became light-headed as my heart beat so wildly I could feel the thumping in my ears. It took a few moments for me to turn towards the house, but there he stood. My husband. Aaron was standing on the porch casually with his hands in the pockets of his pants. It felt as if everyone and everything around us froze while we stared at each other in silence. After a few seconds of eye contact, Aaron descended the steps and walked over to me. He stopped a few inches from where I stood. I reached out to touch him, caressing his cheek and stroking his beard. I opened my mouth to speak but it took several moments before the words finally came out.

"What ... how ... It's you."

"Yeah, mama. It's me."

He took my hand and kissed it. I snatched away from him and slapped him hard across his face. Startled, AJ started to cry in Sophia's arms. Aaron's jaw clenched.

"Venga," Sophia said. She held onto my arm as she tried to usher me towards the house. "Let's go inside."

I didn't move.

"Ma, why don't you go on and take the baby in the house,"

Aaron spoke to his mother, but he kept his eyes focused on me. "Let me talk to Jada, and we'll be inside in a moment."

Sophia reluctantly took the diaper bag and headed into the house. Julio and Danny quickly gathered the remaining bags from the truck and quietly followed Sophia. Aaron reached for me, but I took a step away from him.

"I don't understand what's happening," I said, shaking my head. My emotions caused my voice to quiver. "How is this real? How are you here right now?"

"Jada, there's a lot I need to explain."

"*Explain?* There's no explaining this."

I threw my hands up and stepped around him, headed for the house. I heard Aaron's footsteps while he followed me, and I quickened my pace. Jogging, Aaron was right on my heels when I stepped into the foyer of his family's home.

"Come on, mama. We need to talk about this."

"No," I responded quickly. "I can't."

Aaron took a firm grip of my arm, stopping me from walking any further away from him. He spun me around to face him.

"Let me tell you –"

"There is nothing you can say to make this okay. I thought you were dead!"

Angry tears started to form in my eyes. I pulled away from him and started to walk off. Aaron let out a frustrated sigh and followed me.

"Where are you going?" he asked.

"To find my son."

"Our son," Aaron corrected me.

I stopped in my tracks and turned to face him with danger-ously narrowed eyes.

"Excuse you?"

"Jada, that's my seed. Regardless of whether or not I've been by your side every day, I am his father," he answered firmly. "He is just as much mine as he is yours."

Unable to form a response, I continued to stare at him in disbelief.

"Now look," he said, stepping closer to me. "I understand that you're upset. You have every right to feel every single emotion that you are feeling, but we need to talk, mama. I need to explain all of this. I need you to understand."

I shook my head again.

"I know as the heir to the Cartel you are probably not used to hearing this word, but no," I said in a low tone. "I'm going to lay down."

To my surprise, Aaron didn't follow me when I walked away. My head was spinning, and all I wanted was to lay down. I went up the room – the room I shared with Aaron – where I climbed under the covers of our bed for a nap.

I literally spent the rest of the day in bed. When my eyes finally opened, I was surrounded by darkness. I fumbled around in the dark trying to locate my phone. Once I found it, I saw that it was almost midnight. Sleepily, I rubbed my eyes and noticed that one of the doors leading to the balcony was cracked open. I sat up in the bed and saw Aaron standing on the balcony staring at the water – his back towards me. I released an irritated sigh and ran my hands over my face. He waited all day to talk. Knowing the man Aaron was, I knew there was no more running from the conversation that needed to take place.

I pushed the covers back and rose to my feet. The temperature was so pleasant that I didn't bother to put anything on over the short, fitted tank dress I wore. Barefoot, I stepped onto the balcony and joined Aaron at the railing. He turned to look at me, and our eyes met in the silence. His hair was brushed back into a ponytail, and his facial hair was trimmed to perfection. He was looking better than ever. As much as I wanted to melt into his arms and press my lips and body against his, I resisted.

There was too much anger and sadness within me to be erased by his touch at that moment.

I reached for the glass in his hands. Hennessy on the rocks. I took a long sip before handing it back to him.

"Where is our son?"

"My mother and Dani are watching him tonight."

We stood in silence on the balcony for a few more moments before he spoke again.

"Are you ready to talk now?"

I smirked. "Do I have a choice?"

Aaron shook his head and turned to look at the water before us. He took another sip of his drink before looking back at me. "Jada, none of this was done to hurt you."

"I'm sure you would like to believe that. However, that doesn't change my reality for the last seven months. Regardless of your intentions, I am hurt."

"Everything done was necessary. After the shooting, I was bad off. In my condition there was no way I could protect your or AJ. I had to do what was best at the time which was for me to fall back and heal," he reasoned.

"So, you thought leaving me alone was best?"

"You were never alone. I know it may have felt like it because I wasn't by your side, but in my absence, I made sure that the right people were surrounding you at all times," he responded. "I needed to disappear until I could take care of Michaela Pitt for good. I killed her brother, baby. She was going to remain a threat until I took her out. I needed to be 100% back on my feet in order to get to her before she could get to me. I did that, mama. Michaela Pitt is dead, and there's nothing to worry about anymore. I'm back now."

I found little comfort in his words. Instead, I shook my head and stared at him with a clenched jaw.

"I thought you were dead. Do you have any idea what that did to me?"

Aaron didn't respond. I frowned in frustration.

"Why did you lie?" I continued. "Why couldn't you just tell me what was going on?"

Aaron shrugged his shoulders. "At the time I felt like I couldn't tell you."

"No, you felt like you couldn't trust me," I countered.

Aaron sighed. "Mama, if you knew where I was, I don't think anyone would have been able to keep you from me," he said. "Michaela knew you survived. If she was able to trail you back to me, we both would have been fucked."

"So, like I said ... you felt like you couldn't trust me."

"You were supposed to trust me," he responded firmly.

I raised an eyebrow at his tone of voice.

"If we're going to talk about everything, we need to discuss how the shooting happened in the first place," Aaron stated. "You were never supposed to be at the condo alone."

I stared at him in total disbelief.

"You've got to be kidding me. I know you're not trying to place the blame on me. Ain't no way in hell that's what you're doing right now."

"That's not what I'm saying, but you know you weren't supposed to be there by yourself. You weren't supposed to go anywhere without security, and you knew that," he said. "Jada, I made that very clear to you when we started with all the extra security measures. I asked you if you trusted me. That should have been enough. I shouldn't have had to explain every little detail to you. You were supposed to trust me and follow my lead."

I stood quiet and motionless. Aaron had a point. Although I was unwilling to accept responsibility for the actions of the Pitt twins or Aaron's need to disappear, he was absolutely right. I should not have gone to my condo without Harold and Vic.

But Aaron's months long deception was far worse than my desire to retrieve financial reports from my condo that night.

"Aaron, I understand all of that, but you lied to me for months. That's not okay," I said quietly. "I was grieving and trying to figure out how to take care of our child alone. You had me and everyone else out here thinking that you were dead. What the hell?"

"Everyone wasn't thinking that I was dead," he responded casually.

"What?"

"What?" he echoed my question.

I felt sick while I watched Aaron take another sip of his drink. The implications of his statement made me nauseous.

"What do you mean by that, Aaron?" I asked. "You were dead. There was a funeral and everything. I don't understand what you're saying to me right now."

Aaron shook his head. "Legally speaking ... I was never dead. Someone probably told you something about a small, private memorial service, but none of the news outlets ever confirmed my death. The last media updates listed my condition as unknown. My father and I have connections everywhere. There's no fear of any legal action associated with faking my death, because legally I was always alive."

I felt lightheaded. I paced back and forth on the balcony while I ran my fingers through my hair. I just couldn't believe what he was telling me. I thought back to the day I woke up from my coma – still connected to all types of tubes and wires while I laid in that hospital bed. Everything was such a blur, but I remembered my family being there. I remembered asking about my baby and being told that he was alive and healthy ... but then I remembered how quiet the room got when I asked about Aaron. I couldn't remember who had uttered the words, but I know what I was told. His death ... the memorial service that conveniently took place while I was in a comatose state ... it was all a lie. There were not enough words in Webster's to describe the hurricane of emotions I was feeling.

"Come here," Aaron said, extending his hand towards me.

I shook my head and continued to pace back and forth. After a few moments, I calmed down enough to stop. I stared at him with my hands on my hips.

"I don't understand. Tony said that the finances were taken care of because of life insurance money. I've spoken with our accountant several times."

"Our accountant works for me, and Tony cares for you like everyone else in our families. He was going to say whatever was needed for money to be the least of your worries while you recovered and took care of AJ," Aaron said. "That's why we had him work with the accountant and handle most of your finances anyway. We knew it would go over smoother if you were dealing with someone you trusted."

"We? You just said we twice. Who the hell is we?"

Aaron didn't answer me. He made eye contact with me but took another sip of his drink. However, his eyes told it all. I figured I already knew the answer to my question. I just needed to hear him say it out loud.

"Answer me, goddammit!" My voice was elevated higher than I intended. "Obviously your parents knew because you were waiting for me in their home. Tony knew because he lied to my face for months. Who the hell else knew that you were alive this whole damn time?"

He pulled his glass away from his lips, lowering his hand by his side.

"Come on, mama. I think you already know the answer to that question."

He was right. I did know. There was only one other person alive that would go to such extreme lengths to maintain a lie that was intended to protect me. My stomach dropped at the fact that not only had my husband lied to me for months but that my father had been the one to help him do it. I shook my head in disbelief.

"I can't believe this shit," I mumbled as I stormed back into our bedroom.

Aaron sat his drink down on the balcony table and jogged after me. I snatched my phone up from the bed.

"What are you doing?"

"I'm calling him."

Aaron stood by my side watching silently while I dialed my father's number. The phone rang until it eventually went to voicemail. I shouted a loud curse word before throwing my phone. Aaron took a step towards me, but I shoved him in his chest, pushing him backwards.

"You may not have been around, but he was. He was there the whole time. Every single day! He saw my grief. He witnessed my pain. He even had the nerve to make me see a fucking therapist. The whole damn time he knew you were alive!"

I don't know if the word "betrayed" even scratched the surface of how I felt in that moment. Whatever the feeling was … it hit me like a ton of bricks. Aaron grabbed me, holding me by my arms.

"Every single decision that was made … every single thing I did was for you and AJ," he told me. "It killed me to be away from you this long. This ain't what I pictured when I asked you to marry me, but I had to make sure that Michaela Pitt was wiped off the face of the planet. None of us were safe until I did that."

Aaron wrapped his arms around me tightly, holding me close against his chest. He kissed the top of my head as I buried my face into his chest in an attempt to stop my tears. I was so damn tired of crying.

"I never wanted to hurt you. I just knew that I had to do whatever was necessary to protect my family. I would move heaven and earth for you. I love you more than anything," he said. "You know that, don't you?"

As upset as I was, I did believe him. I nodded as I looked up to see the sincerity in his eyes. With his thumbs, Aaron wiped the tears from my eyes while I leaned in to kiss him. Over the past seven months I had missed him so much that it physically hurt. I didn't want to do anymore talking or anymore explanations. I just wanted him.

I wrapped my arms around his neck and pressed my lips against his, kissing him again. Every angry feeling I had moments earlier had gone out of the window as our bodies became intertwined – hugging, kissing, and caressing each other. I could not pull away from him if I tried. I had missed his touch so much. My body craved him. Aaron lifted me off of my feet, laying me on my back across our bed. Our eyes locked in the darkness while Aaron pushed my dress up to my waist. I raised my hips slightly so he could easily remove my underwear and toss them onto the floor. Grabbing him by his shirt, I pulled Aaron's body down onto mine, spreading my legs so that his body rested between my knees.

Aaron showered me with kisses, starting with my lips and then working his way down my body. Never one to overlook foreplay, Aaron's lips continued further south until they eventually met with my center. While he teased me with his tongue, I was in a daze. He had always been an expert in the bedroom. His oral was no different. As good as I was feeling, it wasn't enough. I had not touched my husband in over six months. I needed more. While his face was still between my legs and his hands gripping my trembling thighs, I begged him to make love to me.

"Are you sure?" he asked looking up at me in the darkness of our bedroom.

There was hesitation in his voice and on his face.

I nodded.

"What's wrong?" I smirked. "It's not like we've never done it in your mother's house."

Aaron shook his head and let out a slight laugh. "That's not what I meant, mama. I'm just asking if you're sure that's what you want right now. You're upset and rightfully so. As mad as you were a few moments ago I just –"

I silenced him with a kiss. When I pulled away from his lips, I slipped my hand inside of his pants, stroking him and discovering that he was already rock hard.

"Baby … all I want right now is to feel the weight of my husband on top of and inside of me," I said, pushing down the front of his pants and his boxes. "Don't you want that too?"

Without hesitation Aaron responded, "Hell yeah."

Aaron quickly removed his clothes before returning to the bed. Laying his body on top of mine he kissed me again and took his time entering me slowly.

After kissing on my neck Aaron spoke directly into my ear. "I missed you so fucking much."

"I missed you too baby."

Aaron gripped my ass as he started to move inside of me harder and deeper making it damn near impossible to breathe. As his stroke became more intense, I felt as if he was pounding away the agony of the last several months. For the moment the tingling feeling running up my spine could serve as a distraction, but I knew that the feeling of bliss was temporary.

AARON

*B*etween the light shining brightly into the bedroom and the Hennessy I drank the night before, I squinted. It was much earlier than I would have liked to be awake. I extended my arm beside me but ended up patting an empty space in the bed. Confused, my eyes quickly opened. I sat up – looking around the room which was still and quiet. A few moments later I heard movement and then watched as Jada stepped out of our walk-in closet. The sunlight that shined around her gave her an angelic glow.

"Good morning," she said softly.

"Good morning."

I pushed the covers back on the bed and stepped back into my underwear before walking over to her. I didn't know how, but she looked even better than the day before. With her back towards me, she stood at our dresser putting on a pair of earrings. I kissed her on the cheek and wrapped my arms around her waist. I frowned when I noticed her body tense from my touch.

"After last night, I wasn't expecting to wake up in our bed alone."

"Yeah ... well I actually have to get ready to go," Jada responded.

I frowned again.

"Go? Go where?"

Jada sighed heavily and turned around to face me. I looked her up and down, surveying her appearance. The curves of her body in the fitted dress she wore were so distracting that I didn't previously notice that her makeup was completely done, and she already had on a pair of those expensive ass stilettos she liked to wear. Her hair was freshly washed – her curls air drying. She had just finished putting on her jewelry. All I could do was wonder where in the hell she was going so early in the morning.

"I'm heading back to Atlanta. I've got an early flight."

"Oh yeah?"

"Yes, Aaron. I just came down here to drop AJ off with your folks for a few days. Your mom and Olivia have been asking to see him. I'll be back at the end of the week to get him, but there's some stuff I need to take care of at home. I need to catch up on work and make a better effort to help Vanessa with some wedding things. I made plans for my week."

"You had those plans before you knew I was back," I told her. I made sure to keep my tone of voice even so that my irritation was not so obvious. "We still have things to discuss. There are things that *we* need to catch up on."

I slipped my arms back around her waist and pressed my body against hers, pinning her against the dresser. For a moment Jada relaxed into my embrace while I covered her mouth with mine and kissed her deeply. I ran my hands up and down her curves and firmly gripped her behind. I could feel her resolve crumbling when she felt my stiffness pressing against her torso. A soft moan escaped her lips. She kissed me back and started to caress my bare chest. I pushed her dress up to her waist and lifted her onto the dresser. I was tugging at her underwear when she tried to pull away.

"Stop," she pleaded breathlessly. I moved my lips from her mouth to her neck. She grabbed my hands to stop me from removing her underwear. "Aaron, please."

My forehead wrinkled into another frown, but I pulled away from her and took a small step back. Jada slid off of the dresser and pulled her dress down before running her fingers through her hair in an attempt to fix her appearance. I noticed that she was still wearing her wedding band.

"For real, Jada?"

"Yes. For real," she answered. She looked down at the Rolex I purchased for her shortly after we began dating. "Julio and Danny should already be outside. I need to go."

"Shit, I can fix that right now," I mumbled. I started to walk towards my phone which was resting on the bedside table. "With Michaela dead and gone, I'm not sure we need to keep Danny on the payroll. He can go back to Atlanta by himself. Julio has been working for this family for a long time. He worked for me long before he ever worked for you. I can send his ass back home right now."

"Don't do that."

I paused with my hand tightly gripping my cell phone. I looked at Jada with an expectant glare.

"Look … I'm not going to lie to you. Last night was … I definitely needed that … "she started.

"But?"

"But staying here in bed with you is not going to fix the issues between us right now. The whole situation is messed up," she said. "You can't just stick your dick in me and make it all better."

"That's not what I was trying to do," I explained. "It's been a long time since I've touched you. Forgive me if I can't keep my hands to myself."

Jada shrugged her shoulders. "All I'm saying is that it's going to take some time to fix this."

"Then don't you think that's time you should be spending here with me?" I asked. "I know we didn't finish our conversation last night, but –"

"I can't do this right now!"

My mouth hung open while I stared at my wife in silence. When I noticed Jada's watering eyes, I figured it was best for me not to press the issue any further.

"I don't think I slept at all last night," she said. "Sometime after you fell asleep, I sat on the balcony just looking at the water and thinking. Thinking about the last several months ... thinking about everyone that's lied to me on your behalf ... thinking about AJ. Our son. I was thinking about the trauma of his first days ... weeks ... months on this earth. I was unconscious in a hospital bed for the first couple of weeks of his life. You weren't there. He was in this world for weeks without being held by either of his parents. I've been battling for months to restore my health and be the best version of myself so I can create a stronger bond with my son and give him the mother he deserves."

I stood still and continued to allow Jada to speak.

"Then I started thinking about something else. I started thinking about AJ's reaction when you came out of the house yesterday. I was confused and my head was spinning, but I clearly remember the way he smiled at you ... like he knew you. He recognized your face and for the life of me I don't know how if you haven't been around."

The look in Jada's eyes was pleading for me to explain, but I didn't open my mouth. She was still trying to process my reappearance. I didn't think she could really handle the truth. She was already so upset with her father. I wasn't sure how she would react if she knew that he would FaceTime me whenever he was watching his grandson. Jada and my mother had such a good relationship. I didn't want to potentially ruin it by telling her that my mother would sneak around to bring AJ to me whenever Jada was in Miami. In that moment, I didn't think I could tell her any of that.

She shook her head in what I assumed to be disappointment at the fact that I did not respond to her revelation.

"Forget it. This whole situation is just too much for me. I need a little space and time to process everything. I need to get back to Atlanta. I just can't. I can't do this. Not right now," she said. She quickly grabbed her belongings. "Spend some time with your son. I'll be back for AJ at the end of the week."

Jada rushed past me and out of the room.

"Jada!" I shouted as she continued to run away.

I followed Jada, but she was moving so fast. I was halfway down the hallway when I realized that there was no stopping her.

"Fuck!"

I watched from the second story landing while she ran down the stairs towards the front door. I turned to look behind me when I heard another bedroom door open at the opposite end of the hall from my room. My younger sister stepped into the hallway with a frown on her face.

"Let her go, Black. She's really been going through it these last several months. I told you that. This hasn't been easy for her. She needs time to process everything," Daniella said. "AJ's still sleep so you need to keep it down ... and put some damn clothes on."

"Yeah alright," I said dismissively while Daniella disappeared back into her room.

I headed back to my room where I grabbed my phone and dialed Jada's number. She let the call go to voicemail. Twice. I shook my head as I pulled the phone away from my ear and stared at it in frustration. Fine. If Jada didn't want to be bothered, then I would let it go for the moment. Instead of trying to reach her again, I called Luke.

"You're up early. What's up, bruh?"

I smirked and shook my head. "I don't even want to get into all of that right now," I told my best friend. "What you got going on today?"

"Not much really. What's up?"

"Let's meet up. It's time to get to work on the shit in Atlanta. The sooner Cameron comes home the better. Hell, it might even put me in better graces with my wife."

"Damn. I figured everything was all good when I didn't hear back from you last night," Luke commented.

"Last night wasn't the problem ... but things got off track this morning. She's headed to the airport right now."

I heard Luke sigh on his end of the call. "Alright, man. I'll be over your way around noon."

After we ended our call, I laid in the bed for a couple more hours before taking a shower and getting dressed. When I made my way down to the main floor, I found my mother, Daniella, and AJ seated at the table in the breakfast nook while our chef put the finishing touches on brunch.

"Dani told me that Jada left this morning."

My mother's tone of voice made her statement sound more like a question. I narrowed my eyes at Daniella. She shrugged her shoulders and looked away from me.

"I already knew that her original plan was to return to Atlanta," my mother said. "I just thought that she would change her mind and her plans once she knew you were back."

"Yeah I thought so too," I mumbled.

"Just give her some time, mijo. She'll come around. If there's one thing I know, it's that she loves you. I'm sure she will be delighted to have her family back together once she's able to accept the circumstances surround your absence," my mother stated.

I nodded in agreement but decided to change the subject. "How's dad?"

I watched my mother as the smile disappeared from her face. "He's upstairs resting. The treatment is really taking a toll on him," she said while she continued to feed AJ. "I know he was anxious to have you back in the middle of things, but I'm hoping that you and Lucas can keep things rolling without him right now. He really should be focused on his health."

"Of course," I said. "Luke and I can handle everything. Besides my family, nothing else is more important than making sure business runs smoothly."

"Good," she said, her bright smile returning to her face. She stood up from the table and picked AJ up from his seat. "I'm going to get this little one dressed and ready for his day. We've got some running around to do, but we'll be back by dinner."

"Sounds good."

Luke arrived shortly after I finished eating and joined me on the veranda. Shaking his head, he pulled the blunt away from his lips before he spoke.

"So, what the hell happened this morning, man?"

I shook my head and sighed heavily. "I don't know. I guess she doesn't get it. She's acting like she can't understand why I had to do what I did. She couldn't know that I had survived or where I was hiding. She's hardheaded. She would have tried to make her way to me and gotten us both killed."

"I know. That's why everyone agreed that your plan was the best course of action."

"I'm not questioning whether or not I made the right decision. I know I did. She's just doesn't understand that right now. Dani and my mom said that I need to give her some time. Jada said she needed time to deal with it all. She can have all the time she wants ... until the end of the week when she comes back to get AJ."

"And then what?"

"Then I'm going to put my family back together. We've been apart for too long to let her emotions continue to keep us away from each other. Besides ... with my father's health condition, she needs to start getting used to the idea of spending more time in Miami. With Julian almost out of game, there won't be much of a need for us to be in Atlanta once Cameron gets out," I responded. "I'm probably even going to sell the house, and she should probably get rid of her condo. I don't even know why the hell she still has it in the first place."

Luke sighed. "Speaking of which ... Julian and PO came to a decision a little bit ago. I didn't bother you at the time, because I knew you were busy on Michaela's trail," he said, "but we know which direction we're moving in now."

"Oh yeah? What is that?"

"Julian and PO have agreed that Cameron won't have anything else to do with the business once he's out. We're free to move forward with working on his release."

I nodded in acknowledgment and took the lit blunt from Luke's hands.

"So, what did you have in mind?" Luke asked expectantly, sitting up in his seat. "I can't imagine that it's going to be easy to get a federal case dropped."

"We've done it before. We just need to do it again," I said, releasing a thick cloud of smoke from my mouth. "Besides ... it's gotta be hard to present a case without two of your star witnesses."

Luke made eye contact with me.

"The girls gotta go, man."

Luke's eyebrows raised. "Both of them?"

"Both of them."

Luke released a deep breath and settled back into his chair. "Dammit, man. I know the end result is that he'll be a free man, but Cam ain't gonna be happy about that."

My face twisted into a frown. "I don't give a fuck. If either

Shannon or the Fed take the stand, he's done. A guilty verdict is going to impact more than just his freedom. It's going to blow back on us and the organization. We don't need any more heat in Atlanta right now, especially with the pending transition. I still need to work with PO to get the mayor and the police chief back on our side," I said. "Cameron created his situation. When you play stupid games, you win stupid prizes. If he really cared about either woman, he wouldn't have them in this position to begin with."

"Say no more, bro. You know I understand. If Nakia got picked up today, there ain't a damn thing she could or would say that would get me jammed up."

"My point exactly."

After the night of the shooting, I was in pretty bad shape. When I was stable enough, my parents transported me back to Miami so that I could continue to recover. Four months later, I was back on my feet and pursuing Michaela Pitt. I had tunnel vision for ninety days until I was able to wipe her off the face of the planet. With that behind us, my priorities had shifted. I needed to reconcile with my wife, get her brother released from prison, and help her father smoothly transition into retirement.

Luke's voice broke into my thoughts.

"How's your pops?"

I shrugged my shoulders. "Mom's putting on a brave face, but this round of treatment kinda has him down. Some days he's up and feeling like himself ... other days he's nowhere to be found. When I got back from handling Michaela, one of the first things he mentioned was stepping down and turning everything over to me."

"For real?"

"Yeah."

"How you feel about that?"

I sighed. "I mean ... I always knew that it would happen one day. I guess I didn't figure how soon that day might be. So much has been going on the last couple of days though. I was just hoping for a moment to breathe ... a moment for things to settle down before I took the crown, but it is what it is. I was born ready, and Pops knows that I can handle it."

"That's for damn sure, bruh. I know you're more than ready ... and you know I'll be right there when it's time," Luke said.

I nodded in acknowledgment. About an hour later, Luke and I were finished discussing business, and he was ready to go. We both stood up from our chairs and said our goodbyes.

"Alright man. I'm going to hit up Uncle Nate and see if we can get a jump on the girl's location. Step one is figuring out where they are in the first place," Luke said.

"Bet. Hit me up when you have some news."

We slapped hands, and then Luke was on his way. I sat back down at the table staring at the perfect ocean view in front of me. My spirit was so unsettled that I could not even enjoy the serenity of my settings. I pulled my phone out of my pocket and sent a text to my wife.

"Take the time you need to process things this week. Don't waste time or money getting another plane ticket. AJ and I will be back in Atlanta this weekend."

Less than a minute later she responded.

"Okay."

I shook my head and let out another deep breath. Her cold shoulder was aggravating, but I knew she would come around. With everything else that was going on, she had to.

PO

"The twins want to spend the night over their friend's house," my longtime girlfriend, Kiara, said. "And Aisha is out with her little boyfriend. I figured we could have a midweek date night if you plan on being home sometime soon."

I held my cell up to my ear and shifted my weight back and forth as I stood outside of the warehouse that served as one of the new meeting spots for the crew. I looked down at my watch and sighed. As tempting as dinner and a movie sounded, I had a meeting that would be starting soon. Several of the guys were already inside. Kiara and I had been together so long that I knew she would understand. The mother of my seventeen-year-old daughter and my twin twelve-year-old girls, Kiara had been by my side through everything major. There were very few people I trusted more than her. Marriage had never been that important to either one of us, but she had been the perfect partner – much like Carmen Reid was for Julian prior to her death.

I spent the majority of my adult life wanting to be like Julian Reid. I had the woman, the knowledge of the game, and the right team in place to handle business. However contrary to what many believed, I was happy that I only had daughters. After witnessing, Deuce and Cameron's demise, I was relieved that none of my children would be following in my footsteps. I could only imagine what Julian was feeling. I had gone over and beyond to keep my girls removed from the life that I lived.

"I got something I need to take care of right now, but I'll be home as soon as I can," I told her.

"Sounds good, babe. I'll be waiting."

I ended the call. It was time for our meeting to begin. It was a Tuesday night, and we were discussing productivity before the end of the week. Before I could head into the warehouse my phone started to ring again. I hesitantly answered the unsaved number.

"Hello."

"Good evening Mr. Oliver," a cheery female voice greeted me. "This is Lauren from Mayor Richardson's office. Do you have a moment to speak?"

Confused by the unexpected phone call after regular business hours I briefly hesitated. "Uh, yeah."

"Sorry to call you so late in the day, but it was a busy day around the office," she explained. "I know this Saturday is New Year's Day, but I was calling to see if you were free for dinner with the mayor that evening."

"Yes. I will definitely make sure that I'm available. Just let me know the time and the place."

"Perfect. I'll let the Mayor know that you will be able to make it. I've secured a reservation for Marcel in West Midtown. Mr. Mercer has already confirmed. Mayor Richardson will meet you both at seven o'clock."

"Mr. Mercer?" I asked.

"Oh, yes! Mr. Aaron Mercer. The Mayor said you knew him. He will be in attendance as well. I hope that won't be an issue."

"Yes, Lauren. I know Mr. Mercer. I just wanted to make sure

I heard you correctly," I said. "Thank you for the call. I'll be at Marcel Saturday at seven o'clock."

"Wonderful. Have a great evening!"

I shook my head while ending the call. I was one of the few people that was aware that Aaron Mercer was alive. I just had no idea that he was preparing to return to Atlanta. We were days away from completing the transition for me to lead the Atlanta organization. With Aaron coming back in town and joining the sit down with the Mayor, I could only wonder what other changes were on the horizon.

I placed my phone back into my pocket and headed into the meeting. Making my way to the head of a long table, I noticed that everyone was in attendance except for two individuals. Julian had chosen to sit out one of his final meetings with the group due to other plans he had for the evening, and Prime was either running late or planning to be a no show. I let out a deep sigh and shook my head. He was really starting to test my patience.

I leaned to my left and quietly asked Zo, "Where is he?"

Zo shrugged his shoulders. "I don't know. I tried to reach him earlier. He just shot me a text not too long ago that said something came up, but he'll get with us later."

"Yeah, I bet."

I sat up in my seat and addressed the room to begin the meeting. Prime would be dealt with in due time. I would make sure of it.

JADA

I laid on my back in the middle of the living room floor in my condo. With my eyes closed, I listened to the music floating through the wireless Bluetooth speakers – some R&B recording artist that DJ recently did production work for. Admiring the melodic sounds of the ballad playing in the background, I raised the blunt to my lips inhaling deeply before blowing out a large cloud of smoke.

"Come on, Jada," Vanessa softly chastised as she walked back into the room, spraying air freshener. "DJ is going to flip his shit if I go home smelling like this crap."

"Double standards," I mumbled with my eyes still closed.

"Excuse me?"

Without sitting up or opening my eyes I responded, "It's okay for him to smoke all day, but he can't even stand you smelling like smoke even though you didn't light up yourself. Double standards, much?"

I heard Vanessa sigh loudly.

"I'm sure you didn't ask me to come over here so we could talk about my relationship. You got back from Miami two days ago. What's going on?"

I rolled my eyes and forced myself to sit up, pulling my knees up to my chest. I reached for the ashtray resting beside me, extinguishing the blunt and sitting it down. I looked over towards my best friend who sat on my sofa with an anxious look on her face. After a few moments without speaking, Vanessa opened her mouth again.

"Jay, what happened in Miami?"

A few more moments passed before I responded.

"Aaron greeted me on his mother's front steps. He's alive."

Vanessa squinted at me in confusion. Several moments passed without either of us speaking. Vanessa had not moved. I'm not sure if she even blinked, but the look on her face was very easy to read. Eventually, the confusion that was etched on her face morphed into disbelief. After shaking her head slowly, I watched as her disbelief quickly turned into anger.

"What … the …. fuck?! You've got to be kidding me!"

I shook my head. "No, Vanessa. I'm not. After leading me to believe that he was dead for the past seven months, my husband is very much alive and well."

Vanessa hesitated again. Taking in a sharp breath, she released it slowly. "Are you okay? What did he say? How in the world did he explain himself? How does he even begin to explain any of this? I just can't ..."

Vanessa continued to rattle a million and one questions as I stood up from my spot on the floor. Turning away from my friend, I walked towards the windows in my living room focusing my attention on the busy streets of Atlanta.

"Jada," Vanessa's voice broke through my thoughts. "Talk to me. How are you doing? What's going on in your head right now?"

I shrugged my shoulders. That was such a loaded question. *How was I doing?* How could I even begin to answer that question if I could not properly label my emotions? I was feeling so many things over the course of the last couple of days that I was almost numb. Almost. The only thing I was really feeling at the moment was anger. *What was going on in my head?* I still had questions. So many questions. Who was going to answer them? Who could I even trust to tell me the truth at this point?

I turned around to look at Vanessa.

"Vanessa, I'm pissed. I'm so mad I literally feel the anger all over my body," I answered. "I can't even comprehend the level of betrayal and the effort that was put forth to lie to me for so long. Who does that? I am his wife. I am supposed to be a part of him ... his rib. How could he hurt me like this?"

Vanessa sat quietly on the couch with her hands in her lap. She didn't have the answers to my questions. She was just as confused as I was.

"Ness, I don't even know what makes me more upset – the fact that he lied or the fact that he had my father help him do it?"

"Your father?"

"He helped him. Both him and Tony. Tony was working with our accountant making sure all the finances were straight but my dad … he was probably behind everything else. He definitely knew that Aaron was alive this whole time. He witnessed first-hand what I was going through and still continued to keep the lie going."

Vanessa shook her head and let out a deep sigh. "Wow, Jada. I don't even know what to say to that. How are they going to get away with all the things they did to essentially help Aaron fake his death?"

"He said he didn't fake his death."

"Huh?"

"Everyone just lied to me," I answered, turning back towards the window. "He was never dead in the eyes of the law."

"Oh, that's some bullshit, Jada! I can't even believe the words that you're saying to me right now," Vanessa shouted. "If you didn't get the answers you need from Aaron, you know exactly where you need to go right now."

I sighed and dropped my head. She was right. I was still angry and unsatisfied with Aaron's explanations. I knew who I needed to talk to – the person who had been around the whole time. The same person who conveniently had not answered their phone since the night I arrived in Miami. Apparently, I had to pop up on my father for our confrontation to take place – a confrontation that I was not looking forward to. My father did not like to discuss business with me, and he did not like to be questioned. I prepared to do both. As close as we had been my whole life, especially since the passing of my mother, only heaven knew if we would be able to get past the betrayal of the past several months.

I turned around to face Vanessa.

"I know … and he hasn't answered the phone since I got to Miami. I was planning on going over to the house sometime today."

Vanessa looked at her watch and then stood up from the couch. "Well grab your purse and come on. I'll drive you."

"What?"

"It's barely ten o'clock. Maybe we can catch him at the house before his day really gets started," she said, picking up her purse and keys. "I'm pissed for you, and you need answers. Let's go."

I hesitated but only for a brief moment. I was dressed, but I had not done my hair or put on any makeup. However, my appearance was the least of my concerns at the moment. I needed to get to the bottom of everything that had happened, and Vanessa was right. My father had all the answers. He always did.

I grabbed my things and followed Vanessa to the front door. After getting into her Audi, I sat in the passenger seat quietly while Vanessa navigated her way towards my father's house. When we pulled into the circular driveway of my father's home several minutes later, I noticed an unfamiliar Lexus parked in the driveway. Vanessa pulled next to the car and shut off the engine. I unbuckled my seat belt and reached for the door handle only to pause when I noticed Vanessa scrolling through her phone instead of getting out of the car.

"Are you coming?"

Vanessa shook her head. "No ma'am. I said that *you* needed answers, and I brought you here to get them. I'll wait out here though. I'm damn near thirty years old, and your dad still scares the shit out of me."

I shook my head and laughed.

"But let me know if you need reinforcement, I'm just a text away," she added.

I exited the car, fumbling through my Louis Vuitton tote for my keys. As I climbed the steps and approached the front door, I heard voices on the other side. They weren't loud enough for me to decipher what they were saying, but my father was clearly speaking to a woman whose voice was oddly familiar. I assumed she was the owner of the Lexus. With my hand still deep inside my purse, I paused just in front of the door as I heard the deadbolt unlock. I wasn't sure if my ears were working correctly until the door opened and my eyes confirmed what my ears had heard.

"Thanks again for breakfast. Now that I know I can trust your cooking skills you can feed me anytime," Dr. Sandra Peterson said as she caressed the side of my father's face and planted a kiss on his lips.

I stood there motionless on the front porch while they were obviously oblivious to my presence and focused on each other. While my father kissed my psychiatrist, I observed her appearance. The skirt and blouse she had on was an outfit she would have worn to the office. Between her wrinkled and untucked blouse, the flip flops that were on her feet while her heels were in her hand, and her messed up short-cropped hairstyle, I could only assume that Dr. Peterson had come to my father's home for much more than pancakes and bacon.

"Wow," was all I could manage to say while I stared at them in disbelief.

They both turned to look at me for the first time with matching looks of surprise on their face. My father was the first to speak.

"Jada, what are you doing here?" he asked. "I thought you were in Miami with –"

"My dead husband that's not really dead," I interrupted him, looking at my therapist. I addressed her directly. "I would ask if he told you that Aaron was alive but seeing as how you're here … looking like that … well, I guess I can only assume that you were in on the lie the whole time."

Dr. Peterson's face fell into a frown. "Jada, it's really not –"

"Lady, don't stand here and tell me it's not what I think," I said calmly, shaking my head. "I've already been lied to enough. Please don't insult my intelligence too."

A tight smile forced its way onto Sandra's face as she made

eye contact with me. "Well then. I think that's my cue to leave. Julian, I'll talk to you later."

I refused to move, forcing Sandra to awkwardly step around me before she made her way to her car. My father had a look of frustration on his face while releasing a heavy sigh.

"Come inside so we can talk."

I shook my head. "No. I wanted to talk the night I got to Miami and found Aaron alive and breathing at the Mercer's estate. I wanted to talk any of the times I've called your phone since then and even on the drive over here," I said. "But now ... after seeing you with the therapist you had me see to keep up this inconceivable lie ... now ... I don't want to talk at all."

I turned on my heels and headed back to Vanessa's car without my father attempting to stop me. My guess was that he knew it was a lost cause.

AARON

The week had passed by quickly. I attempted to call Jada a few times only to be met with voicemail. To be honest, I wasn't that bothered by her silence. I allowed her to have her time to be upset while I got back into the swing of things with business. With my father's health taking a toll on him, there was much more on my plate than the transition and issues happening in Atlanta. I needed to be in Miami more often than not. The quicker I could handle the situation in Atlanta and reconcile with my wife, the better off I would be.

It was New Year's Eve, and also the end of the week Jada needed to herself. AJ and I were back in town. I settled into my seat in the Escalade while Danny drove towards my destination. I assumed that Jada would be at her condo but was surprised when I got there and discovered it was empty. Frustrated, I told Danny to head towards the house in Sandy Springs. I was tired and so was AJ who slept peacefully in his car seat. I didn't have the energy to hunt Jada down.

"You sure you don't want me to try to call her?" Danny's voice broke into my thoughts.

"Nah man. Just drop us off at the house and go spend the

evening with your family," I responded. "I appreciate you picking us up from the airport."

"Whatever you need."

I closed my eyes and relaxed against the headrest while Danny continued our drive. Several minutes later, the vehicle slowed down as we approached the security gate for my neighborhood. After gaining entry into the development, Danny navigated the vehicle to our street. When he pulled into the driveway, I sat up straight in my seat and narrowed my eyes in confusion at the lights that were on. Surprisingly, Jada was home.

The moment Danny brought the car to a stop I unbuckled my seatbelt, grabbed my son and headed right to the front door. I heard Danny speak to my back while he said that he would bring the bags into the house. I didn't stop to acknowledge him. I quickly entered the house to see lights on throughout the first floor – great room, kitchen, dining room, but Jada was nowhere to be found. Careful not to disturb AJ, I made my way up the stairs and towards the master suite. As I started down the hallway, I could see dimmed light coming from the cracked bedroom door, and I heard the faint sounds of R&B music playing in the background.

I paused briefly – a little uneasy because I had no idea what was on my wife's mind. We had barely spoken all week, but there she was waiting for me in our bedroom. I had no idea what I was walking into.

"Mr. Mercer."

I turned to see Julissa coming down the hall to meet me. I frowned, even more confused. She and Jada didn't always see eye to eye.

"Let me take little AJ and get him settled," Julissa said, taking my son from my arms.

"It's the holiday, Lissa. What are you doing here?"

Julissa smiled warmly and kissed AJ on the forehead. "My

family is out of town. It was no problem for me to come in tonight. It's good to see you back, Mr. Mercer. I know Jada will be glad that you are home."

I sighed. "Yeah. I don't know about that," I mumbled.

Julissa smiled again and patted my cheek. "Trust me," she said before turning and heading towards AJ's room.

After another brief moment of hesitation, I headed for my bedroom. I slowly pushed the door open to see Jada, standing by the fireplace in the sitting room – her back towards me. She was dressed in a black satin and lace negligee with a long, sheer matching robe and another pair of the expensive ass stilettos she loved that accentuated her toned legs. I paused in the doorway admiring the view.

"Welcome home."

Jada turned to face me. Her makeup was flawless and although her face was gorgeous as always, her eyes looked sad and tired. She walked across the room to me, pulling me inside the room by my coat and closing the door behind me.

"How was your flight?" she asked, wrapping her arms around my neck.

I pulled her body closer to mine – gripping her narrow waist firmly with both hands. I kissed her lips.

"It was fine. Uneventful. AJ was pretty calm," I answered. "Honestly, the whole week was pretty smooth. I was eager to get back to you … but I have to say that I wasn't expecting this type of homecoming."

Jada cocked her head to the side and looked at me quizzically. "What were you expecting?"

I shrugged my shoulders. "Jada, you ran out of the house the other day, and we didn't speak much this week. I didn't know what I was coming home to."

Jada sighed but took my hand. She started back towards the sitting room, pulling me along with her. "I don't want to talk about all of that. It's New Year's Eve. Let's just enjoy the evening and each other while we celebrate the New Year – a new beginning."

I followed Jada to the sofa, sitting down beside her. On the table in front of us was a charcuterie board, a bottle of champagne in a bucket of ice and two glasses. Jada held my hand, interlocking her fingers with mine. The only light in the room came from the glowing fire and a few lit candles. I was appreciative of her romantic efforts, and she looked breathtaking in the dim light of our bedroom. Looking at her reminded me of the night I first saw her, the night of Shannon's birthday, when I first came to Atlanta to help Julian's team while he cared for his ailing mother. In the middle of that dark night club, Jada captured my attention and ultimately my heart. The last thing I wanted was to be at odds with her.

I raised her hand to my lips and kissed it softly. She smiled at me weakly and then pulled her hand from mine in order to pour our glasses of champagne.

"You don't know how happy I am to be back. I just want us to be able to move forward, mama. It's important to me that we are okay with all the other changes that are on the horizon," I told her, sipping my champagne. "I really just want –"

"We don't have to get into all of that right now."

"Jada, I –"

"Please," she said, sitting her glass of champagne down on the table. "You literally just got home. You haven't been here … with me … in our bedroom for months. I don't want to talk about business or changes on the way or Michaela Pitt or any of that shit tonight."

I closed my mouth while Jada took my glass from my hand and set it next to hers. She eased her way onto my lap, straddling me and once again wrapping her arms around my neck. Her robe fell off of her shoulders, exposing a scar on her shoulder from one of the bullet wounds she sustained from Mikey Pitt. I brushed my thumb across the scar before kissing the spot. Jada shrugged away, pulling the robe back up. Pushing me back against the sofa, she pressed her body and her lips against mine, kissing me deeply.

"I'm glad you're back, babe. I really don't know if you understand how much I really missed you ... but I don't want to sit around talking all night," she said with a mischievous grin. She winded her hips, slowly grinding on top of me. "I'd rather do something else with my mouth ... something I know you like ... something I know you've been missing for months."

I only considered her proposition briefly before deciding how I wanted to spend my evening. I scooped her up in my arms as I stood up from the couch. Jada giggled loudly when I hoisted her over my shoulder, smacking her ass and carrying her to our bed. Conversation could wait until tomorrow.

PO

I took a sip from my glass of water, placing it back on the table before looking over at Mayor Dwight Richardson. As he casually scrolled through his cell phone, I looked at him, sizing him up. The man sitting before me in his custom-fitted suit stood all of five foot eight – considerably shorter than Julian, Aaron, and myself. Had it not been for his high-profile political position in the city, I otherwise would not have considered this man to be a threat or intimidating to at all. However, word on the streets was that due to his upbringing in the inner city, he had been familiar with people similar to Julian and me for years. Although he was a widely regarded attorney prior to taking political office, it was heavily rumored that his entanglement with people on the other side of the law dated back several years. Given the relationship he and the police chief shared with Julian, I was persuaded to believe the stories I had heard.

Mayor Richardson looked up from his cellphone as our waitress reappeared at our table.

"Mr. Oliver … Mayor Richardson … are you ready to place your orders?"

"Not yet. We're still waiting on our other party. He just told me he is on the way. If you could give us a few more minutes, he should be here shortly," Mayor Richardson responded with a friendly smile.

"Sure thing."

After the waitress left our table, Mayor Richardson sat his phone down, slightly leaning closer to me as he rested his forearms on the table.

"So, PO, it may be courtesy to wait until Aaron gets here to order our food, but there's no reason why we can't start a conversation. I'm sure you're a busy man like me and have other things to attend to today," he said with a tight smile. "So, Julian tells me you've been his right hand for years. Is that so?"

I nodded. "It is. We've worked together for many years. Over twenty to be exact. I've been his number two for the last ten or twelve years."

"Wow. Ten years, huh? That's a mighty long time to sit at the right hand of the person on the throne."

I shrugged my shoulders in response. I was interested to see where this conversation was headed. Mayor Richardson took a sip from his glass of water before he continued to speak.

"I take it you had a front row seat to the mayhem that ensued during the battle with KS9?"

I nodded again. "Sure. You could say that."

"Then it should be no surprise to you how things have gone off course with the arrangement that your organization had in place with the powers that be at City Hall," he stated.

"KS9 was a different kind of beast," I responded. "The reason we had the issues we had with them is because the leader of their crew used to be a part of our team. He knew things about how we operated that no outside enemy would have ever known. You can imagine why it may have taken a little longer to get rid of them."

"Dissention amongst the ranks?"

"It wasn't quite like that," I answered. "Caleb Bridges hadn't been a part of our team for a while."

"But yet he still had enough inside knowledge to cause the type of commotion that we agreed to keep off of the front pages of the newspapers," Mayor Richardson commented.

Instead of responding, I took another sip of water. To be completely honest, I wasn't sure if he was anticipating an answer. His statement sounded like a question, but the look on his face told me he already had his mind made up. He didn't really care what I had to say, and I wasn't sure what the point was of our meeting.

"Here's the thing, Patrick," the mayor started. My jaw clenched. No one ever called me by my government name. "It's no surprise that I am aiming to expand my political aspirations. When my time as mayor is over, I am looking to take my talents to the national stage. It's a little hard to prove myself worthy if I can't make it appear that I have a handle on the drug trade and violent crime in my own city – my hometown. Julian and I worked well together for a while, but you can see how things have transpired over the last couple of years. I understand you're the one in charge now, but you've been around Julian and his organization the whole time. Why should I believe that anything would be different with you steering the ship?"

I smirked and fixed my glare on the mayor. I sat up straight in my chair, leaning towards him as I cleared my throat to speak. I had spent years proving myself on the streets – years at the right hand of the man who had controlled the drug game in Atlanta and taught me everything that he knew. If Julian was good enough to conduct business with the mayor, then so was I. I would be damned if I begged this man for anything. Sure, it would be easier to make the moves I needed to make with City

Hall on my side, but I didn't get to where I was by kissing ass and I wasn't about to start with him.

"Let's get something straight, Dwight," I stated. "You don't know –"

"Gentlemen, sorry for my late arrival."

I broke eye contact with the mayor as we both looked up to see Aaron approaching the table. He had a friendly smile on his face as he pulled out a chair and sat down – momentarily oblivious to the tension at the table. When he looked from the mayor's face to mine and then back to the mayor, the smile slowly faded and was replaced with a more serious look.

"Why do I feel like I'm interrupting something?"

Before I could respond the pensive look on the mayor's face disappeared as he forced a tight smile and spoked. "Just a conversation amongst new friends," he said, patting me on the back.

Aaron's eyes drifted towards me for nonverbal confirmation of the mayor's comment. However, he could read the look on my face to mean that Dwight Richardson and I were nowhere near being friends. He sighed heavily.

"I see you two started discussing business without me, huh?"

Mayor Richardson shrugged his shoulders. "We were both here. I figured why not make good use of our time."

"Uh huh," Aaron said, casually looking at the menu instead of looking at either one of us.

Our waitress approached our table again. "Mr. Mercer, I see you made it. Are you all ready to order or will you need a few extra minutes?"

"I actually won't be staying long, but if you could give them a few more minutes I would appreciate it," Aaron answered.

I raised an eyebrow as the waitress silently retreated. Aaron just arrived several minutes late and was planning to leave our meeting early.

"I hate to cut and run but family and business call," Aaron

explained. He set the menu down and looked at us. "Since you started without me, I suppose we can jump straight to the point of our meeting."

"Prior to your arrival, PO and I were just discussing the challenges the team has faced over the last year or two. Aaron, you're a sound businessman. You can see how a continued relationship could be concerning to someone in my position."

Aaron nodded but didn't respond. The mayor continued to speak.

"My business arrangement worked out well with Julian for years, but the recent heat brought to the new papers and eleven o'clock news is detrimental to my future goals. I understand you and I have not worked as close together as I have with Julian, but I'm a strong ally to have in this city. Along with having the protection from investigations and prosecutions when the chief of police and other agency heads are in agreement, it's beneficial to have me on your side."

"I hear you," Aaron said. He stroked his beard as if he was deep in thought. "It just sounds like you're not willing to give my man here a fair chance because of one or two unfavorable situations that have occurred even though you yourself stated that you had a successful, and might I add lucrative, partnership with Julian Reid for years. Being the sound businessman that you say I am, I can't find the logic in that. Why would you want to walk away from the type of money that you've been accustomed to receiving for years?"

The mayor leaned back in his seat, folding his hands in front of him.

"I admit that the money was an excellent benefit to the partnership, but I have to assess the risks of staying involved with your ... *crew*. I have to ask myself if staying in business with your team is worth the potential damage it could cause to my political future. True, I was in business with Julian for years, but how do I know that PO can bring to the table what Julian once did. I mean look at this latest situation with Julian's son. Cameron is still in federal lockup. He's facing major time for the very types of crimes that I need to distance myself from in the public eye. If we are going to continue working together, I damn near need guarantees that there won't be any more issues like KS9."

"Guarantees? And how do you suppose we do that? I've never known anyone who has been able to predict the nature of our business," Aaron stated.

"Well I know no one at this table is a fortune teller, but Aaron, if we are going to move forward then somehow someway you and your partner here need to make me feel a lot more comfortable with the direction that the team is headed in."

Before responding, Aaron paused to read and respond to a text message he received. He slipped his phone back into his pocket, sitting up in his chair and leaning a little closer to both the table and Mayor Richardson.

"You sure are using the word 'if' a lot."

The mayor's face fell into a questioning frown. "What do you mean?"

"You've used the phrases 'if we are going to continue to work together' and 'if we are going to move forward'. Mr. Mayor, you're almost making it seem as if you're the one holding the cards in this situation," Aaron said. "Almost as if you can easily choose to walk away from the agreement that's been in place at any time you see fit."

"I beg your pardon?"

With my elbow resting on the table, I covered my mouth with my hand to hide the smirk on my face. I didn't have to be the one to tell the mayor about himself. Aaron seemed to be handling that all on his own.

"What I'm saying is this ... Julian Reid has done business with my family for longer than he's known you. You are quite aware of who I am and who my father is. You know what my family is all about. When you decided to do business with Julian, you also agreed to do business with my family. You don't get to just throw your hands up and say that you're done. You don't walk away from the Cartel that easily."

Mayor Richardson's smile remained on his face, but his eyes narrowed while he glared at Aaron. "Are you threatening me?"

Aaron shook his head and laughed.

"Of course not. I am merely relaying the facts of the situation. You've never been the one with the power. This arrangement is beneficial to all parties involved, and it's important to me as well as my father that it continues. Keep in mind ... you and I might not have worked together that closely, but I know all about you. All about your past. All about the illegal things you've been involved in since your high school days at Carver. You could say that I know where all the bodies are buried ... and how do you think that information could potentially affect your *political aspirations?*"

"What are you trying to say?"

"I'm saying that I know you have connections and could have intervened to prevent the investigation into Cameron Reid. Your failure to do so has created a sizable headache for me that I'm not too pleased with. I don't want any more headaches. So now you're going to talk to your police chief friend and find a way to get him back on board with the arrangement that was previously in place."

The smile finally dropped from the mayor's face.

"Or what?"

"I don't think you want to know the answer to that," Aaron said, standing up from the table. He reached into his pocket to pull out a couple of large bills and dropped them onto the table in front of the mayor. "I'll leave the two of you to figure out that steps needed to move forward. Dinner is on me. PO, we'll talk soon."

Aaron turned to walk away without another word. Mayor

Richardson silently stared at me as our waitress approached the table again. Hesitantly, the mayor placed his order and I followed suit assuming that our conversation would continue in Aaron's absence.

Once the waitress was out of earshot, the mayor took another sip of his water and then looked back at me.

"So where should we start?"

JADA

I slowly spun around in the center of the room while I took in my surroundings. I accompanied Vanessa to look at her top choice of wedding venues. With my peripheral vision, I could see Vanessa looking at me expectantly, with a wide smile and her hands clasped in front of her. The building was very industrial in appearance with interior brick, exposed pipes, and hardwood floors. The space was nice but not what I envisioned Vanessa choosing for her wedding day – the day she had been dreaming about since we were twelve years old.

"So, what do you think?" Vanessa's voice echoed throughout the room.

"It's cute."

Vanessa frowned. "You don't like it?"

"It's not that I don't like it. I just thought you were more of a ballroom at the Biltmore type of girl. This just wasn't what I was expecting."

"The thing I love about this is the ambiance," Vanessa said, "and it's pretty much a blank slate. The decorator can do all types of things with this space. Look at some of the pictures from previous weddings that held here."

Vanessa handed me her cell phone, and I scrolled through the screenshots in her photo gallery. Each picture showed a wedding ceremony more elaborated than the last. I was floored to see how the venue had been transformed for each of the occasions. Maybe Vanessa was on to something.

"Well what do you ladies think?" a voice behind us asked.

Vanessa and I both turned around to see a venue employee with a wide smile and the same expectant look Vanessa had for me moments earlier.

"I love it," Vanessa beamed.

"That's wonderful!" the young lady exclaimed. "Are you ready to review a proposal and possibly start a contract?"

Vanessa glanced down at her watch. "I'm waiting on my fiancé, but he should be here any minute."

"No problem. I'll be in the back. Just let me know when he arrives. I'll be more than happy to show him around and go over a few quotes for you both."

Vanessa smiled in response while the woman retreated. I handed Vanessa's phone back to her.

"I didn't know DJ was coming," I said. "You're pretty serious about locking this place down, huh?"

"I am. We placed a deposit on another venue, but our date became available here due to a cancellation. This is my first choice, and I know the date won't stay open long," she said. "If DJ likes it, I want to do a contract today."

"Wow. That's awesome," I said with a warm smile. "It's crazy how time is flying. Your big day will be here before you know it."

"I know. I can't believe it," Vanessa said. She changed the subject and asked, "How's everything been going with Aaron? Is he still here?"

I shook my head and sighed. "Nope. Left this morning,"

"For how long?"

I shrugged my shoulders. "Who the hell knows? He said he'll

probably have to be down there for a while with everything going on and his dad. He wants me and AJ to come back down there to spend some time together as a family. I'm not really interested in being in Miami right now, but I guess I have to be fair. When he came up here for New Year's he was only supposed to be here for the weekend, but I ended up getting him to stay for three weeks."

"And how did you manage that?"

I laughed and gave Vanessa a sneaky grin. "With some Agent Provocateur and these double D's," I said, pointing to my chest.

Vanessa shook her head and laughed at me. "Keep it up and AJ and Olivia will have another sibling."

We both laughed loudly. A few moments later, we were interrupted by the sounds of two males conversing. I looked over my shoulder towards the entrance, my laughter halting when I saw who had joined us. DJ had arrived, but he wasn't alone. He was joined by his business associate and rapper, Malik. The same Malik I had been involved with for months before meeting Aaron. Although Malik was close friends with my best friend's fiancé, I had not seen him in quite some time, and his presence took me by surprise. DJ greeted me quickly before walking over to Vanessa. Malik paused where he was, his eyes lingering on me, before making his way over to where I stood.

"Hey," he said.

"Hey."

"Long time," he said.

"I know."

Malik reached in for a hug, and I allowed him to embrace me. He slowly pulled away but held onto my hand for a moment.

"You look good," he said.

"You too," I admitted. "How have you been?"

"Good. Real good. Getting ready to drop another album

soon. I was actually just leaving the studio with DJ, and he asked me to bring him over here," Malik responded. "What about you? I was sorry to hear about what happened to you … and your husband."

"Yeah well. We're doing fine now."

I noticed Malik's eyes drift down to my left hand, the one that he was holding. I wasn't wearing my rings. I pulled my hand away.

"*We're* doing fine?" Malik asked. "I thought I heard that he –"

"No. He's alive," I answered. "He was down bad for a minute, but he's doing pretty well now. Back at a hundred percent. Back on his feet."

"Damn. That's what's up," he said. "I'm glad to hear it."

"Thank you."

The words that came out of his mouth stated that he was glad to hear about Aaron's recovery, but I picked up on a look in his eyes that indicated that he may have been disappointed at the fact that I was not single. Before Malik or I could say anything else, Vanessa approached us.

"Hey you two," she said. "DJ and I are going to be awhile. Malik, he said you can take off. He's going to ride home with me. Jada, I'll try to get through this as quick as we can, so I don't keep you waiting too long."

"Y'all rode up here together?" Malik asked.

I nodded.

"Yeah we did," Vanessa answered, "and actually now that I think about it … since you're about to take off, do you mind dropping her off at her place? Her condo's not too far away from here. No more than twenty minutes or so."

Malik looked at me but answered Vanessa. "I remember," he said. Something about the familiar look in his eyes caused my stomach to become unsettled. "Works for me. I'm cool with it if she is."

I paused. I probably wouldn't have hesitated if I hadn't

noticed the brief look of disappointment in Malik's eyes moments earlier when he realized that Aaron was alive. Something about being alone with him made me uneasy, but I quickly brushed off the feeling. I knew that Aaron had slightly lightened up on the security measures now that the Pitt twins were deceased. However, he would not be thrilled to hear that I was hanging out with a guy I used to date. I considered declining Malik's offer and waiting for Vanessa and DJ, but instead I told myself I was reading too much into things. I accepted the ride.

"Alright, girl. Call me later. I want all the details," I told Vanessa, giving her a brief hug.

"Of course."

Vanessa headed back towards DJ, her heels clicking on the hardwood floors as she walked away from us. I turned to look at Malik who had a grin a mile wide on his face.

"You ready?" he asked.

I nodded. "Ready."

AARON

I sat on the edge of the desk in my father's office looking back and forth between Luke and my Uncle Nate while they conversed. There was so much on my mind that I was only half listening to their conversation until Uncle Nate addressed me directly.

"Aaron, I've been working on locating Cameron's girls," he said. "Luke already told me about the plan. Seems like the best thing to do. The quicker we can get him out, the sooner we can be finished with all that shit in Atlanta."

I sighed. "Tell me about it."

"I'm pretty close to locating his girlfriend," Nate commented.

"Which one?" Luke asked, shaking his head.

"His main girl. Not the Fed."

"We probably need to find the Fed first though," I stated.

"Why is that?" Nate asked.

"Shannon knows a lot, but the DEA agent has more damning information," I responded. "She was at our spot. She saw our faces. Shannon knows a little bit, but I guarantee you the Fed is going to be the one to make the case."

Nate shook his head. "This shit is ridiculous. Who knew that Cameron Reid was such a goddamn fool?"

"Shit, we found out during the time we were up there in Atlanta," Luke answered.

"Don't make no damn sense," Uncle Nate stated. "I would have expected much more from Julian's son."

"Apparently Deuce was much better at handling things than his dumbass kid brother," I said. "I don't know what happened with Cameron."

"Well at least he has agreed to step away from the business," Nate commented. "That's going to be best for everybody."

"Agreed?" Luke asked. "I don't think he really had a choice. When I ran the options by PO and Julian, it seemed pretty obvious they came to the agreement for him."

"By choice or by force. It doesn't make a difference to me either way," I said. "All I care about is the fact that I don't have to worry about him fucking anything else up."

"I know that's right," Uncle Nate said, standing up. "Look, I'm going to go on and get out of here. I'll get some folks onto finding the Fed. I should have both locations soon."

"Sounds good. Let me walk you out."

Luke followed while Uncle Nate and I headed towards the front door of the house. After he left, we headed to the veranda. Luke and I both took a seat facing the water. I never got tired of the view of the Atlantic Ocean from my parents' estate. He pulled a lighter and a rolled blunt from his pocket.

"So, how's your pops doing man?" Luke asked as he put the lit blunt to his lips and inhaled deeply. He passed it to me.

I shrugged my shoulders. "I can't call it. One minute he's fine and on top of the world. The next day he's not even getting up out of the bed."

"Is he still talking about hanging it up and handing shit over to you?"

"Yeah, he's been talking about it. I don't know if he's really ready to do it though," I answered. "Running the business ... living this life ... this is all that he knows. If he ain't doing this, what else is he gonna do?"

"Your guess is as good as mine. Our dads came up in this shit together. If my dad was alive, I know he would still be at your dad's right hand. This is what we were raised to do. There ain't no plan B," Luke said. "This shit is in our blood."

"I know man. I was just thinking the same thing."

"The real question is not if your dad is ready to hang it up though. The real question is ... are you ready to take it over?"

I shrugged my shoulders but didn't immediately respond. I raised the blunt up to my lips with my right hand while looking down at the wedding band on my left.

"You know I can do this shit in my sleep. Ain't no question on whether or not I can run the business. I've been groomed for this shit," I answered truthfully. "But it's not just about me anymore."

"I know man," Luke said as he took the blunt back from me. "How is everything going on the home front? You stayed up in Atlanta a lot longer than you were supposed to. I assume everything is good now?"

"I can't call that either, man. There's an obvious disconnect between me and Jada right now. She's still not speaking to her father over the whole situation. It's like she's happy that I'm back, but she's built up these walls and ain't trying to talk about anything that matters – nothing of importance. She don't want to talk about the last several months or anything happening in the near future. I'm trying to make sure that she and I are in a good place before I even try to talk about me taking over for my dad. Shit's tough, bro. I'm trying to repair what was messed up, but them walls she put up ain't coming down. Anytime I try to talk about anything important she changes the subject or tries to distract me with sex. All she wanna do is fuck."

Luke looked at me in disbelief. "And that's a problem?" he asked as he started laughing. "You're like the only nigga in the history of niggas that I ever heard complain about getting too much ass."

I shook my head and laughed as well. "Bruh, that's not what I was saying," I responded. "I ain't touch my girl for months. Of course, I'm trying to be all over that, but she doesn't want to talk about anything important – anything heavy. That shit just don't make sense to me. What woman do you know that doesn't want to talk?"

"Damn my nigga. You're right. Shit, lately I can't get Nakia to shut up," Luke laughed. "Every time I walk in the door it's something else."

"Naw, man. Me and Jada ain't never really had those problems. She's never been the type to stress me. We've always been able to talk through any issues or problems. She's my sounding board, bruh," I responded. "We're a unit. Since the day we met, I've always felt connected to her. This shit going on now isn't sitting right with me. It just doesn't feel right when we're not in sync."

Luke leaned back in his seat digesting my words. "Damn Black, I ain't never heard you talk about a woman like that."

"She's not any other woman, bro. She's my wife. Even at our best, I never considered putting a ring on Isabela's finger. That should tell you something right there," I responded. "Even after Olivia was born, we never talked about marriage. I loved Isabela, but it didn't even compare to what I feel for Jada. She changed the game, bruh."

"Then you need to do whatever you gotta do to make that shit work," Luke stated in a matter of fact tone. "Whether your dad makes up his mind today or three years from now, the throne is gonna be yours. When that happens, you're gonna want everything to be cool with you and your wife. What's a king without his queen, bruh? Handle that shit."

LUKE

TWO MONTHS LATER

Zo sat back in the passenger seat of the pick-up truck, slightly shifting the AR 15 pistol that sat on his lap.

"Aye, man. Where's your boy at?" he asked. "I'm ready to get this shit over with."

I laughed. "You ready to get this over with? Or you ready to get down to Miami for a few days?"

"Both, but I'd be lying if I said I wasn't ready to hit South Beach. A nigga needs a vacation," he said with a laugh of his own. "Big time."

"But how's your girl going to feel about you skipping town for a few days to go to Miami solo?"

"Which girl?"

"Your wife, nigga."

We both laughed, and Zo shook his head.

"Courtney's fine. That ain't the one I'm worried about," he said, still laughing. "Alana been applying pressure lately. She's been all in my shit. I need this break bad, bruh."

I shook my head and laughed again. I was about to speak when I noticed a dark figure in dark clothes headed our way.

"Aye, here this nigga go right here," I said, sitting up a little straighter.

The rear passenger door opened, and Marquez, my hitter from Miami, slid into the backseat. I glanced at him over my shoulder and watched him pick up the assault rifle that waited for him. He sat it on him his lap, inspecting it in the darkness of the vehicle.

"What's it looking like, man?" Zo asked.

"They had more agents last night. Don't make no sense to me, but whatever," Marquez answered, shrugging his shoulders. "It's one out front in that unmarked sedan. Just switched out with another nigga like an hour ago. Four total agents inside with Shannon, including the other girl y'all want to get rid of."

"They got ol' girl in there with her?" Zo asked with a surprised look.

I nodded.

"How the hell you know all this?" Zo asked.

"I know things," Marquez answered simply.

Zo looked at me for further clarification, but I just shrugged my shoulders. "He's one of Uncle Nate's protégés. He knows things. That's why he's up here."

"So anyway," Marquez continued to explain the plan to Zo. "The back is clear. So y'all gonna pull to the next street over and cut through to the back yard. I already scoped the area. Ain't no real security. Only real surveillance is on and in the safe house. I'mma give y'all enough time to get into position and then kill the power. They dumb asses ain't got no back up. I'm gonna roll up on the car. Pop that nigga and then head inside. Luke got the floor plan memorized. Follow him inside once you hear the shots. Get this shit over with and then get the fuck on."

"Well shit," was all Zo could say. "Alright then."

"See y'all niggas inside," Marquez said.

I cut the engine on while Marquez hopped back out of the truck. Through the shadows, I could see him headed towards the outside power connection to the house – seemingly preparing to cut the power just like he said. I pulled the truck over to the next street, leaving it in the driveway of a run-down, abandoned house. Zo and I hopped out of the truck with our weapons and cut through the back yard of the abandoned house, making our way to the backside of the safe house. We hid behind a few bushes staring at the back windows of the house until we saw the lights shut off.

"Game time," I said.

Zo followed my lead while I quickly made my way up to the back door. A few moments later, we heard the sound of gunfire coming from the front of the house. I waited three seconds and then shot the lock off the back door. Entering the house from the front and the back blocked off both exits and sent the agents in different directions. Zo and I rushed into the kitchen to hear more gunfire coming from the front. I started towards the living room until Zo pulled me back after hearing movement in the hallway. A split second later, the hall bathroom door flew open and an agent came out with his gun in his hand. Headed towards the front of the house, his back was towards us while Zo and I stepped out of the kitchen.

He started to turn in our direction but never had the chance to pull his trigger.

Zo and I both fired our guns dropping the agent's bullet-riddled body to the ground. I led the way to the living room, pausing on the opposite side of the staircase from Marquez. I could see the bloodied body of another agent lifelessly laying on the steps. Two agents down. Two agents plus Shannon to go. Marquez nodded in my direction.

"The rest upstairs," he said. "I got it down here."

"Bet."

Zo and I slowly and quietly made our way up the steps. Once

we reached the top, we split in separate directions, checking rooms one by one. After leaning close to one of the closed doors, Zo took a step back and shot through the door multiple times, dropping a body on the other side. At the sound of the gunshots, I heard a gasp on the other side of the door I stood outside of followed by another voice shushing the person who gasped. Zo pushed the door open to the room he shot into, quickly looking inside. Satisfied that he had taken out another agent, he looked towards me. I waved him in my direction, confident that the last two occupants of the house – Shannon and Agent Kendra Franklin – were hiding in the master bedroom.

"Got them both. They're in here together," I said.

Zo nodded and then kicked the door open. We entered the room with our weapons raised. When we stepped inside, Kendra raised from the other side of the bed shooting her Glock 17 in our direction. Dodging her bullets, Zo fired at her, striking her in the chest and arm. She fell onto her back dropping her gun. We walked over to see her huffing – struggling to breathe while blood rushed from her arm. The impact from Zo's shots to her bulletproof vest knocked the wind out of her. I raised my gun, shooting her in the head and putting her out of her misery. I turned to look at Shannon who screamed into her hands which were covering her mouth. Tears were filling her eyes. I shook my head at her.

"I'm sorry," she cried. "We can forget all of this. I don't have to testify. I swear I won't do it."

Zo smirked and shook his head. "Too late for that, sweetheart."

"Yeah," I said. "What he said."

I aimed my gun at Shannon shooting her once in the chest and once in the head. I turned towards Zo, who had already tucked his gun under his arm.

"Let's get out of here," I said.

"Yeah. Just one … last … thing."

I raised an eyebrow in suspicion as I watched Zo pull a bottle of liquid out the front pocket of his hoodie. I hadn't been paying close enough attention to notice it before.

"Bruh, what the fuck?" I asked.

"Burn it down. Destroy any evidence," he said.

I just shook my head and laughed while Zo started to pour whatever accelerant he had on the floor. He waved me towards the door, and we started back down the steps – Zo steadily pouring the whole way down. Marquez started laughing. I just shook my head and shrugged my shoulders before he could even ask.

"When I drop this match, run like hell," Zo said.

As soon as Zo ignited the fire, we all took off, rushing out the back of the house to the truck waiting one street over. I hopped in and started our drive. My job was done, and it was time for me to get the hell out of Atlanta – hopefully for a while. We headed straight towards the airport – all three of us eager to get to Miami. Ditching the truck in the parking lot of a train station, we met up with one of PO's dealers – giving him strict instructions to get rid of the guns before he gave us a short ride over to the airport where the Mercer's private plane was waiting.

The next afternoon I sat in a jewelry store looking at the engagement ring I held in my hand, examining it from all angles. I wasn't the flashiest guy, and I didn't own a lot of jewelry. It wasn't my thing. Diamonds never really impressed me much, but I knew the ring I held was going to accomplish my goal. It was sure to take Nakia's breath away.

"What do you think about this one, Mr. Malone? Is this the one?'

"Yeah. This is it," I told the sales consultant before handing the ring back to her. "Excellent choice, Mr. Malone," she said with a wide smile. "Let me get this cleaned again, and I'll have you all ready to go. I'll be back with shortly."

The sales consultant practically skipped to the back. I'm sure she was calculating her commission along the way. I felt Aaron's hand slap my shoulder as he leaned closer to me.

"My boy, you sure you ready to take that leap?" he laughed.

I smiled and said, "Yeah, man. Why not? Nakia's the one so it's time to go on and lock it down. We damn sure ain't getting any younger."

"Shit, don't I know it," Aaron said. "I'm glad you'll be joining the club though. Now you'll get to see what married life is all about."

I laughed. "Enlighten me, brother. I know we've been busy with work, but how's everything been with Jada?"

Aaron sighed but maintained the smile on his face. "You know we went to Cabo last month for our anniversary, and I thought that might be a turning point but ain't shit changed really. Jada's still taking her clothes off to dodge serious conversations, and she's started drinking again. A lot. She's aware that my dad really isn't improving, so it should only be logical what is going to be on the horizon. I just haven't had the opportunity to say it," he answered. "I knew it was going to take some time to fix things, but shit … I didn't know it was going to take this long. She still ain't really speaking to her father either."

"Still?"

"Still."

"Damn man. I hope they patch things up quick. Once Cam's out, y'all probably gonna be moving back here, right?"

Aaron shrugged his shoulders. "That's the plan. I just have to let her know. I'm sure she'll still be in Atlanta from time to time, but I want my family under the same roof for the majority of the time," he said. "She's so hellbent on keeping that damn condo of hers so I'm going to get rid of the house. You know I'm still having one built down here. It should be finished soon."

"I'm sure everything will work out," I told him.

"Yeah. We'll see," he responded. "Anyway, let me know when you are thinking about getting everybody together to celebrate the engagement. Regardless of the shit we have going on, I'm sure Jada will want to be in town for that."

"Definitely. It'll be soon for sure. I know Nakia won't be able to wait after I give her that damn thing," I laughed. "When's Jada planning to be back in town?"

"Within the next week or so, but I don't know how long she's going to stay. I'm sure she'll want to be back in Atlanta once her brother gets out."

"I bet."

After the sales consultant returned with the ring, I completed the purchase. Aaron and I headed out of the store towards our vehicles.

"Aye man," Aaron laughed while he shook his head. "Y'all burnt that shit down last night?"

I laughed. "That boy Zo is wild, man. That nigga don't give a fuck."

"I know, man. That's why I wanted him to be PO's right hand. He doesn't hesitate. He's down for whatever," Aaron said, "but he's smart as fuck and rarely makes mistakes. He's going to be important for the future of Atlanta."

I nodded while we reached our vehicles and went our separate ways. Aaron was right. Whatever the future held for Atlanta; I knew Zo was going to be a major part of it.

JULIAN

I released a deep sigh as I took a break from looking at the computer screen while I sat in the back office of JR's Body shop. The body shop was one of the several legit businesses I still owned after severing my business ties with the Cartel. I had spent the afternoon reviewing financial statements, and I was ready to call it a day. Before I could shut down the computer, there was a knock at my door.

"Come in."

The door slowly opened, and PO stepped inside.

"Hey, man. What brings you by?" I greeted him.

"Just came by to kick it for a minute. Just stopping by to see how everything was going," he said, closing the door behind him and sitting down on the other side of my desk.

"Perfect timing," I said. "My eyes were starting to cross looking over all of these damn numbers."

"Yeah, I bet," PO joked. "But for real … how has everything been going?"

I shrugged my shoulders. "Everything has been good. Who knew how much I could increase profit margins with the businesses when I actually focused on running things in a legit way?"

PO and I shared a laugh.

"That's good shit though," PO said. "You're a true businessman. You've always excelled at whatever you put your mind to. How's the fam?"

I sighed. "Ayanna's doing well, but the other two ..."

"I heard that Cameron's legal team requested to move the trial date up," PO responded.

"They did. Without either of the star witnesses for the case, the Feds probably don't have enough to make the charges stick. They expect he'll be out pretty soon," I answered. "Of course, I'll be glad to have him home, but you and I both know he's going to need some time to adjust to the new normal. After Deuce passed, I'm sure he assumed that he would be the one to fill my shoes one day."

PO nodded in response. "How's Jada?"

I sighed again. "Still not speaking to me," I responded while I shook my head. "Not really anyway."

"Still?"

"Still."

"Damn Julian ... it's been over three months," PO said.

"Yeah, I know. Look, I don't blame her for being upset, but I still stand by the decisions that were made. We did what was best for her and her family. Her husband was able to handle his business and return back to her safely," I answered. "I gave her some time and some space to get over it. It's been long enough."

"I hear you, man. Y'all have always been close, and life is too short for that."

I agreed. "What's going on with you though? How's everything going in your world? I heard things are supposed to be back on track with the mayor now."

"Something like that," PO answered. "Aaron pretty much told his ass to fall in line. He's still trying to assert some sort of power by saying that we can revisit the previous agreement on a contingent basis so he can assess how I run my business. He said he doesn't want any problems like the shit with KS9 or the Pitt Twins."

"Have y'all had any issues?"

PO shrugged his shoulders. "Not really. Not any big ones like KS9."

I nodded, but I knew there was something that he wasn't saying. I had worked with PO for several years. I knew how to read between the lines with him.

"PO, you know better than anyone how small problems can lead to big problems if they aren't handled early. What's going on?"

"This nigga Prime."

"The young boy that took over Ryan's old trap?"

"Yep. That one," PO responded in a frustrated tone. "He's the only one that's been a problem since the transition of leadership. He's been doing his own thing like there aren't rules. He shows up to meetings when he feels like it. He misses money drops when he feels like it. Now I'm hearing that he might be trying to put on some of those niggas from New York that you and I shut down a few years ago."

"And why are you tolerating any of this shit?" I asked with a frown. "We never put up with shit like that before. Niggas get one chance to fuck up – not three."

"We just getting back in good with the good folks over at City Hall. You know that New York crew rolls deep. I don't know what type of war that might start if end up going toe to toe with them and Prime. I've been trying to maintain the status quo," PO answered with another shrug of his shoulders.

"Maintaining the status quo is how we got Caleb Bridges, man. You need to handle that shit. Motherfuckers don't get to call their own shots. What the fuck does he think this is?" I asked.

I leaned back in my chair and looked at my former right-hand man. The man who had been by my side conducting business for over two decades. The man that often made moves off of intuition because he frequently knew what I was going to say before I said it. I didn't think this time was any different, but if he needed to hear me say it, I would.

"He's gotta go."

PO nodded. "Yeah I know."

"The sooner the better too," I continued. "He's already fucking up by trying you for everyone to see. The last thing you want this early on is for niggas to think they can try you. You know that. You need to make an example out of his ass for that alone. That shit is unacceptable."

"Some people just have to learn shit the hard way," PO said, "and dammit if it ain't one thing it's another. Now I gotta find someone to replace his ass."

"You'll find someone," I said in a matter of fact tone. "PO, if I had any doubt that you could handle this, I would have never turned shit over to you. You know what to do. Just do it, and fuck what the mayor has to say. I promise he doesn't want any issues with the Mercers. If Aaron told him to honor the agreement, you don't have anything to worry about. Make the moves you need to make."

"Bet."

PO hung around for another hour before heading out. After shutting down for the day, I packed my things and left the shop. I planned on heading home for a quiet evening, but halfway into my drive I decided to make a detour. Soon, I pulled into a parking space in front of Ayanna and Jada's salon. The words shared between PO and myself rung in my ears. I had given Jada plenty of time and space, and life was entirely too short to allow this to continue. I shut off my engine and exited the car.

Although the salon was scheduled to close within an hour, it was still very busy. I stopped at the front desk.

"Hey Mr. Reid," the receptionist greeted me. "Ayanna and Jada are in the back."

"Thank you."

I passed her desk and made my way down the side hallway that led to my daughters' offices and storage. I heard their voices coming from the supply room. As I approached the opening, I paused in the doorway. Ayanna noticed me first.

"Hey daddy," she greeted with a wide smile as she walked over and hugged me.

Jada did not smile or move from the shelf she was stocking. "What brings you by?" she asked.

"We need to talk, and I knew I would actually be able to catch you here today," I answered my younger daughter.

Jada looked at Ayanna with narrowed eyes and mumbled, "I wonder how you knew that."

Ayanna shrugged her shoulders with an innocent smile. "Well, I'll leave you two to chat. I need to make sure they're wrapping up so we can get out of here at a decent time tonight."

Ayanna took off down the hallway leaving Jada and I alone in silence. I stepped inside of the stock room and closed the door behind me. Jada walked away from the shelf and took a seat on a nearby step stool.

"No hot date with Dr. Peterson tonight?" she asked.

I sighed and shook my head. "Jada, we have bigger issues than your therapist. Let's talk about what's really going on."

"Finding out you were fucking the therapist you made me go see because of a big ass lie kind of is the issue, Dad."

"I admit the optics look bad, but Sandra and I were dating before you started seeing her. That's actually why I was able to get you in to see her so quickly."

"Is that supposed to make the situation any better?"

"No. I suppose not, but Jada, the only reason you found out about her is because you came to the house to talk about Aaron that day. So, let's talk."

"There's nothing to talk about anymore," Jada said with a shrug of her shoulders. "You and Aaron did what you felt you needed to do so he could get himself together to slay the evil dragon known as Michaela Pitt."

"Yeah, but –"

"There's no but. That's exactly what happened, right? You two decided to lie to me for months, because you thought that was best for everyone."

"Jada, I –"

Jada stood up from her stool. "Dad, it's simple, isn't it? I'm just supposed to shut up and go along to get along while everyone else determines what's best for my life … like I'm not a grown ass woman," she said, "but that's what I signed up for, right? That's life as the wife to Aaron Mercer."

"Jada, we made the right decision," I clarified. "What you need to realize is –"

"No. I don't –"

"If you would just shut your mouth and let me finish what I'm trying to say," I said with a raised voice, cutting her off just as she had done to me.

Jada's eyebrows raised at my tone of voice, and she placed her hands on her hips. Yes, she was a grown ass woman, but I was still her father. I had given her more than enough time to come around. I understood that she was upset by the things that happened, but I was not about to let her stand in my face and disrespect me no matter how old she was.

"First, you need to remember that I'm the parent regardless of how old you are. I didn't tolerate disrespect when you were a child, and I'm not going to allow it now," I told her. "Now, everything you said is true. Aaron needed to heal, and we collectively decided that it would be best if you did not know what was going on. Jada, you have a track record of ending up in the middle of situations you don't have any business being in, and you're hardheaded. You wouldn't have listened to me or your husband, and that might have gotten you both killed. Aaron probably won't say it to you, but your stubbornness and poor decision making is what caused the shooting to begin with. We weren't going to take another risk like that when Aaron couldn't be around to protect you. So yes, we made a decision in regard to what needed to take place, because we – at least I – could not trust you. We did what was best."

"So … it was best for me to be to walk around grieving for months unable to give my son the mother he deserved?"

"Would it have been best for AJ if he ended up an orphan due to your actions?"

Jada's hands remained on her hips while she glared at me with a clenched jaw. Subtleties never got through to her. I had been her father for twenty-nine years. I knew how to get my point across to her.

"Exactly," I said. "Jada, what was best for you is what was best for everybody – including your son. We were all impacted by the damage Michaela caused. Losing either one of you would have caused a traumatic chain reaction for both families. It's important that you know that. It's also important that you understand who you are now. You're not just my daughter. You're not just AJ's mom. Jada, one day Aaron is going to take over for his father, and that day may be sooner than you think. When it happens, you're going to be the wife to one of the most important men involved in the drug trade in North America. You won't get to call the shots. Aaron loves you, and he will always consider your feelings. However, you're going to have to accept that sometimes decisions will be made for you. That's not to hurt you or belittle you, but it's because you don't know everything. There's no way that you could."

Jada didn't respond so I continued to speak. I wasn't done getting things off of my chest.

"It seems like you're starting to realize all of this though, because it's obvious that you've forgiven your husband," I said, "and what I don't understand is how you can forgive one and not the both of us."

"Because it's not the same," Jada said quietly. As much as she tried, she was unable to keep the emotion out of her voice. She dropped her hands by her side and looked down at the ground, shaking her head. A few moments later, she looked up into my eyes, her own eyes glistening. "The betrayal I felt from you is worse. I've always been a daddy's girl – even more so after mom died. The fact that you could sit back and allow me to go through that ... I can't even ... I don't understand how any parent could watch their child suffer like that."

I didn't have a response for her. In Aaron's absence, I had made sure that I kept a close eye on her. I was the one that practically forced her to see Sandra in the first place. Yes, it had been a rough couple of months, but it had been necessary to make sure that she and Aaron were safe.

I cleared my throat before I spoke. "I don't want you to think that it was easy for me to see you like that, because it wasn't. Still ... if I had to go back and do it all over again, I would make the same decisions," I said. "Jada, it's pretty obvious that we are going to have to agree to disagree on this in order to move on."

"Yeah you've got that right."

"If you're unable to see from the viewpoint of the two people who love you the most, then you'll never understand why we did what we did," I told her, "but even when you're pissed off at the both of us, you know deep in your heart how much we love you. Even if you don't agree with the method, you should understand the intent."

"I know you love me, Dad. I've never doubted it."

"Then can we just move forward? Please."

Jada shrugged her shoulders and said, "Yeah."

She walked over to me and embraced me in a halfhearted hug. "I need to finish up here, but I'll call you or stop by the house sometime soon."

I nodded. Jada walked past me, opening the door and heading back to the front of the salon. The conversation did not go the way I had hoped, but it was a start. At the very least we could start to work on things, and then hopefully she would come around.

JADA

I stood in the large walk-in closet of our bedroom at the Mercer estate wondering why in the world I had so many clothes there. I spent the majority of my time in Atlanta yet my side of the closet in Miami was almost full. That made my decision-making process much harder as I tried to figure out what to wear to Luke and Nakia's engagement party. Dressed in my undergarments, my makeup and hair were already complete. The sooner I decided on my dress and shoes the sooner we would be ready to go. I heard Aaron's footsteps before he appeared in the closet, stopping by my side and kissing me on the cheek.

"Damn mama, you not ready yet?" he asked. "Julio's probably outside already."

I shrugged my shoulders and smiled at him while I looked at his appearance. He was dressed in all black – fitted slacks, button-down, Gucci loafers. His thick, wavy black hair was loose and resting on his shoulders. He had allowed his facial hair to grow out and although it was trimmed neatly, his beard was full. He looked so good I had half a mind to ask him if he wanted to skip the party.

"Perfection takes time," I said.

"Bullshit. You're always flawless," he said, winking at me. "I'm gonna check on the kids. Can you try to be ready in the next ten minutes?"

"Yes sir."

Aaron kissed me again and left me alone in our closet. I heard my cell phone ring but ignored it. We were already running behind. I needed to decide on an outfit quickly. I chose a black Alexander Wang midi slip dress, which I was pulling on when I heard my phone ring again. I ignored it a second time opting to select my shoes for the evening. My leopard print Manolo Blahnik sandals were in my hands when my phone rang a third time. Wondering who in the world was trying to reach me I jogged back into the bedroom grabbing my phone right before it went to voicemail.

"Ayanna?" I answered the phone.

"Hey Jada, where are you?" my sister asked. "Are you still in Miami?"

"Yeah. I'm getting ready to head to a party," I answered, sitting on the edge of the bed while I started to put my shoes on. "You tried to reach me a couple of times. What's going on?"

"It's Shannon," Ayanna replied.

"What about her?" I asked with a deep frown. "I haven't spoken to her since Cameron was arrested."

"Apparently she's been in protective custody waiting to testify for the trial," Ayanna said.

"Figures," I mumbled standing up from the bed.

I walked over to the full-length mirror to check my appearance. I was so disappointed to hear that Shannon was a witness for the prosecution. I learned that she was so upset about Cameron cheating on her that she agreed to work with the Feds. I was shocked because regardless of Cameron's actions I knew that they really loved each other. I had hoped that she would change her mind before the trial.

"Yeah well her mom showed up at the salon today fussing and causing a scene," Ayanna said.

"About what?"

"Something happened about a week ago that the Feds were trying to keep quiet. Apparently, the safe house was set on fire. They are still working through their investigation, but it doesn't look like anyone made it out," Ayanna answered. "It looks like Shannon and the agents with her are dead, including the one that Cameron was messing around with."

"Damn that's fucked up, but why was Shannon's mother at the salon?"

"Because she's convinced our family has something to do with it."

"What?"

"The Feds haven't said that directly, but they are definitely leading her to believe that. It's obvious that foul play involved."

"And she thinks we would be behind it," I said. "Yanni, that's a bit of a stretch. Don't you think?"

"I don't know, Jada. If there is foul play involved, it would make sense that someone connected to Cameron would be involved," Ayanna answered.

"Okay. Did you ask Dad?"

"No ..."

"You were thinking that I would?" I asked. "Yanni, we're speaking again, but I'm not about to ask him that. If you want to know, you ask him."

"No, Jada. I was thinking you could ask Aaron."

"Excuse me?"

"Come on, Jay ..." Ayanna started. "Dad's out of the business now. Shannon's mom is alluding to someone killing her daughter while in federal protection. If a move of that magnitude was going to be made, you know the Mercers would be involved."

I was quiet for a moment. Ayanna was making sense. Part of

me wasn't sure I should get involved, but there was also a part of me that wanted answers.

"Jada, are you going to ask him?"

I paused when I heard our bedroom door open.

"Yanni, I gotta go," I said. "I'll call you later."

I quickly ended the call, pulling the phone away from my ear. My mind was racing from my conversation with my sister. My father and my husband had made a point to never directly discuss their business with me, but this was different. This was about family.

"Aye mama, you finished?" Aaron asked. "My mother has the kids settled so I'm ready if you are."

I didn't respond, but I turned around to look in his face. Before I could stop myself, the words spilled out of my mouth. "Where's Shannon?"

"What?"

Something within me begged me not to repeat my question, but I could not remain quiet. I took a deep breath to steady my voice before I asked my question again. "Where is Shannon?"

Aaron's face hardened, and he released a deep breath. He closed the door to our room behind him.

"Why are you asking me that?" he questioned in a low and even tone.

"Because I want to know," I responded. "Shannon's mom heard about some safe house fire or some shit like that and she showed up at the salon asking Ayanna questions."

Aaron shook his head and shoved his hands deep into the pockets of his slacks. He stared at the ground for a moment before looking back up at me. "The only reason you're asking me that is because you suspect I had something to do with whatever may or may not have happened," he said, "but you know I don't discuss my business with you."

My face wrinkled into a frown. He and my father were starting to sound like broken records.

"Your business? This isn't about business, Aaron. This is about family. She's practically a member of mine. I want to know what happened."

"Correction she *was* practically a member of your family, but that changed the minute she decided to testify against your brother. Like I said ... I don't discuss my business with you," he repeated himself. "Your father never included you in the business and neither will I."

His unwillingness to deny that he had knowledge of the circumstances surrounding Shannon confirmed that he did in fact know what was going on. My stomach became unsettled.

"I am not one of your children. You are my husband and I –"

"And my job as your husband is to love, provide for, and protect you." His voice was elevated and stern. "That does not mean that I am obligated to share the details of how I go about doing that."

He paused for a moment, releasing another frustrated breath. He walked further into the room until he was standing right in front of me. He removed his hands from his pockets and took mine in his. In a much softer tone, he said, "Now look, the goal is to get your brother home ... and there was an obstacle in the way of me doing so. I took care of that. It's kind of hard for the prosecution to present a case without their star witnesses and a bunch of circumstantial evidence. A problem needed to be solved, and I handled it. That's all you need to know right now."

My heart dropped as a wave of nausea threatened to arise. He kissed my right hand.

"Now," he said. "Grab your things and let's go. Julio already has the car pulled around front."

All I could do was nod in response. I picked up my Louis Vuitton clutch and followed him to the Escalade that awaited us. Aaron held the door open, assisting me into the vehicle before he got in on the other side. Before Julio could even pull out of the gate, Aaron was on the phone talking to someone about something else business-related that did not concern me. I turned away from him.

Staring out of the window as we headed towards our destination, I silently wondered if this was the life that my mother had lived. I knew that she and my father were very much in love. There wasn't a single day that I questioned that. However, I wondered if she was a spectator to her own life, not able to question or be in the know about things happening around her – things that affected her. I wondered if she ever felt that her role as the wife of a powerful and important man was to shut her mouth and raise the kids. Did she ever feel like she existed as an arm piece to see and be seen but not heard? My parents were young when they married – younger than Aaron and me. I wondered if my mom knew the life she was agreeing to when she decided to become Mrs. Julian Reid. Was she okay with it?

I thought about Aaron's words from the night he proposed to me.

"You broke the mold, mama. The fact that you're still standing after all you've been through proves how tough you are," he said. "Tough enough to handle your businesses, your family ... even tough enough to call me on my shit. You're caring and compassionate and loyal. You've opened my heart in a way I never thought it could be opened again."

I didn't feel tough. In fact, I felt powerless – nothing like my old self. Nothing like the person I was before I agreed to be his wife. I felt removed from my businesses, some of my friends ... even some of my family. The days of "calling him on his shit" were long gone. I felt like some of the key qualities he once loved about me no longer existed.

Still on the phone, Aaron grabbed my hand and held it in his lap, giving it a gentle squeeze. I'm sure it was meant to be reassuring so I offered him a smile. Although a weak one, it was the best I could manage at the time. He winked in return and continued to speak on the phone.

A short while later, we arrived at the venue for Luke and Nakia's engagement party. Putting on my best smile, I forced myself to be as social as I could be by using one too many glasses of champagne as a distraction to drown our conversation from my mind. After a couple of hours celebrating the happy couple, I lost count of the number of champagne flutes I had downed. As I reached for another glass, Aaron appeared by my side. He pulled the flute from my hand and sat it back on the waiter's tray.

"Excuse me ladies," he said to Nakia and her friends with a pleasant smile. "I'm going to steal my wife for a moment."

He ushered me away from the group until we were out of earshot of the chatting group of women.

"I was going to drink that," I told him.

"I think you've had enough," he said evenly. "Matter of fact, I think it's time for me to get you home."

"The party's not over."

"Yeah but you've had enough fun," he told me. He placed his hands on my waist and pulled me closer to him. Whispering into my ear he said, "Besides, you're looking good enough to eat in that dress, Mrs. Mercer. I'm trying to take you home so we can have our own fun."

After saying our goodbyes, I let Aaron steer me out of the party. Julio was waiting outside for us, and it didn't take long to get back to the Mercer Mansion. It was well after midnight and the house was dark and quiet when we entered. Aaron's hands were all over me before we could even make it up the stairs to our room. I welcomed the distraction. Despite my best efforts to drown her out of mind, I was still thinking about Shannon.

And I didn't want to.

Instead, I wanted to be consumed by the tangled mess of arms and clothes we became as we hastily made our way into the bedroom. We undressed each other in a hurried rush. In a matter of moments, I was lying on my back across our bed in nothing but my underwear. Aaron hovered above me, kissing me from my ear to my collarbone. His trail of kisses lingered at my neck while he removed my thong and massaged my clit with his thumb. I welcomed the river of wetness between my thighs. Aaron was always eager to please me – even when we were sloppy drunk and both ready to feel each other. He raised his body slightly and placed his hands on my knees as he gently spread my legs and moved his head between my thighs. He proceeded to tease me with his tongue until I was squirming underneath him and calling his name.

"Come here," I breathlessly beckoned him.

When his lips met with mine, I wrapped an arm around his neck and kissed him deeply. I used my free hand to release him from his underwear stroking him slowly and gently.

"Dammit, Jada," he mumbled as he pulled his lips away from mine and kissed my neck.

Using both hands and my full body weight, I pushed Aaron onto his back. In the darkness of the room, I could see the smile tug at his lips when I straddled him. I lowered my hips, mounting him slowly as a soft moan escaped my lips. I rocked and rolled my hips to a slow and steady beat riding him like a prize-winning cowgirl. Aaron's hands massaged my butt and thighs while he licked and then bit his bottom lip. Eventually, I increased my pace from slow and sensual to a passionate, more intense rhythm. Aaron's hands traveled up to my waist where he tightened his hold on me. When I lowered my hips he would forcefully raise his to meet mine. With one hand on his chest and my other hand gripping his shoulder, I struggled to keep my composure. Aaron always knew how to find my spot. When he was inside of me, it was impossible for me to think about anything else. The champagne from earlier and the touch of my husband had silenced the earlier thoughts of Shannon that had been flooding my mind. I was thankful.

When we were finished, I laid on my side – my back against Aaron's chest while he wrapped an arm around my waist. I was ready to drift off to a peaceful sleep. Aaron kissed my bare shoulder and spoke into my ear.

"Look … I'm sorry about earlier. I wasn't trying to be dismissive, but I need you to understand something … this life that we are living will be a lot easier for you if you know less about the ugly details," he said. He tightened his hold on my waist and sighed. "I know that you and Ayanna got close to Shannon over the years so this may be tough for you. It's a tough situation period, but Shannon should have known what she was signing up for when she decided to get seriously involved with someone like your brother. There's a certain loyalty that is required to be a part of this family. You know that, Jada. Disagreements will happen. We won't always see eye to eye … but you can't go against the family. She should have known that there would be a consequence for that."

It was not lost on me that he continuously referred to Shannon in the past tense. Reality was setting in.

"It takes a certain type of woman to be able to deal with a man like your brother … your father … me. There are no guarantees in this life that we live. I pray it doesn't … but this could all end tomorrow. Shannon wasn't the type to still be by Cameron's side when things got bad. We have to ask ourselves if it all came crashing down tomorrow would the women in our lives still be there. I've never had to ask you that, because I already know the answer, mama. You were cut from a different cloth."

He kissed my cheek.

"I just need you to know that I will always do whatever it takes to protect our family and our livelihood, and I won't ever apologize for that. Making the tough decisions keeps food on the table and a roof over the head of the ones that I love, and you know how much I love you, right?"

I nodded.

"I'll do anything for you, Olivia, and AJ."

I nodded again. "I know, baby. I love you too," I said as I closed my eyes tightly.

Sleep couldn't come soon enough.

CAMERON

The first thing I noticed when I stepped out of the prison was that the April sky was the most gorgeous shade of blue I recalled seeing in sometime. A smile stretched across my face as I admired the beauty above. There wasn't a single cloud present. I closed my eyes and took in a deep breath. Something about the feeling of inhaling the fresh air as a free man for the first time in almost a year put my soul at ease. I wanted to savor the moment.

The second thing I noticed was my sister, Jada, standing outside of a black Escalade that was waiting for me. Despite the warm smile on her face, the smile faded from my own face. The peace I felt moments earlier quickly faded. I had hoped our father would be the one to pick me up. Jada was the last family member I wanted to see. However, I made my way across the pavement to where she stood.

"Hey!" she greeted me. "How does it feel to be up outta there?"

She wrapped her arms around me for a tight hug. I embraced her loosely with one arm.

"Shit feels good," I answered truthfully. "If I never saw this building again, it wouldn't hurt my feelings."

"I hear that," Jada said, still smiling at me. "Come on. Let's get out of this hellhole."

She didn't have to tell me twice. I opened the door to the Escalade. Jada hopped in and slid across the bench middle row. I slid in next to her. She introduced me to her driver/security, Danny, before he started driving.

"Where are we headed?"

Looking over a text message she had just received, Jada distractedly responded to me. "Dad's house. You know he got rid of your and Deuce's houses while you were away. You can crash at either of our places until you pick out a new spot," she answered. "Your barber is going to meet us at Dad's, and Yanni is bringing you some clothes. Some people are getting together a little later at the house for food and drinks."

She paused to look up from her phone.

"I hope that's okay …"

I shrugged my shoulders. It didn't make any difference to me. As long as I got a hot shower and a haircut, I didn't care what else the day held. Having a house full of people would be a good opportunity for me to distance myself from Jada anyhow. There was a conversation we needed to have, but I would have preferred for it to happen another day. I shifted my body in my seat, relaxing and staring out of the window.

The rest of the ride to our father's house was quiet, except for a couple of phone calls that Jada answered. One call was from Vanessa and I heard her say that she was planning to come by later. She answered another call where I heard a male voice asking if she was still free later, but I knew it wasn't Aaron. She kept the call polite but short telling him that she was busy with family today but would call him back later. I silently wondered who that could have been and questioned if her husband knew other niggas were calling her phone. I shook my head and continued to look out of the window. That wasn't my business.

When we pulled up to my father's house, there were several cars already there – some familiar and some not. I hopped out of the truck, heading towards the house without waiting for Jada. The door was already unlocked and let myself into the house to a host of waiting family members including my father, Ayanna and her family, Aunt Vita, and Aunt Jackie and her family. I greeted them all with hugs. My father introduced me to Sandra, the woman he had been dating for months. When Jada finally entered the house, I observed how Jada awkwardly interacted with our father and purposely avoided Sandra. I made a mental note to get that story from Ayanna before the day was over.

After taking a long, hot shower and getting my hair lined up, I was ready to rejoin my family. When I made my way back downstairs more family and friends had shown up. It felt good to be surrounded by loved ones after being locked up for almost a year. I walked into the kitchen with my niece, Katy, on my hip, stopping at the refrigerator in search of something to drink when I heard a familiar voice.

"Hey, Julian. What's good, man?" I overheard Aaron Mercer greet my father.

My jaw clenched as the two engaged in brief small talk. I grabbed a bottle of water for myself and a juice for Katy. After sitting her down, I urged her to go find some of the other kids. I walked around a few other family members in the kitchen to approach my father and my brother in law. Their conversation ceased in my presence.

"Cameron, it's good to see you're home," Aaron said.

He extended his hand. I ignored it.

"It's good to be home," I said evenly.

I raised my bottle of water to my lips and took a sip. Aaron smirked and stuck his hand into his pocket.

"Alright," Aaron said. "Have you seen Jada?"

I shrugged my shoulders. "That's your wife, man. I'm not her keeper."

My father's head turned in my direction with a questioning look on his face. I didn't make eye contact with him. He turned back towards Aaron.

"I think she's in the basement."

"Thanks, Julian," Aaron said with his eyes still on me.

When Aaron disappeared, my father turned back towards me and asked, "What was that all about?"

I shrugged my shoulders again. "We ain't never been friends. He doesn't need to put on fake it now."

My father shook his head, but I walked away before he could say anything further. I joined a couple of my cousins in the family room where they were watching a basketball game. Several minutes later, Jada stormed into the room, her heels clicking furiously. She walked right up to me.

"We need to talk."

I looked at her with a stone face. "Can this wait?"

"No."

I sucked my teeth and let out a frustrated sigh. "Come on, man. Shit."

I stood up from the sofa and headed towards the French doors that lead to the back patio of the house. Jada followed closely behind, slamming the door shut behind her. Before I could speak, she was addressing me with fire in her eyes.

"What the fuck is your problem?"

"What do you mean?"

"Cameron, you've been rude as shit since I picked you up, and I didn't know where your head was at so I excused your attitude towards me, but you've got some nerve to show your ass in front of Aaron," she spat.

I shook my head and laughed. "Aaron? You worried about why I acted some way towards Aaron?" I asked. "The same nigga that put me in an early retirement? The same nigga that took out both my girls?"

Jada's face relaxed from the tight frown that had been present.

"Seriously Cameron? That's what this is about?"

"What else would it be about?"

Now I was the one with a frown on my face. Jada shook her head at me.

"He had to do what he had to do to get you out of prison. Would you rather still be behind bars?" she asked.

"If he's as good as everyone thinks he is, he could have found another way."

"Or you could have never cheated on Shannon to begin with. That girl loved you, and if you never would have –"

"So, I'm to blame for everything your husband has decided to do while I was locked up?" I asked.

"Cameron, you getting locked up put a microscope on the very operation that keeps a roof over our heads. Your charges were dropped. You weren't acquitted. It's only logical that you might still be watched after your release. Why risk your freedom again?"

"You sound just like that nigga," I told her. "It's nice to know what side you chose."

"What?"

"You heard what the fuck I said."

Jada's eyes were narrowed, and her hands were on her hips. "There ain't no sides, Cameron. We're all on the same team. Maybe you were forced out of the business because your ass still can't see that."

"The operation here in Atlanta may roll up to your husband and your in-laws, but Aaron and I were never on the same team," I told my sister. "Since the minute Dad went to care for Nana, Aaron was against everything I ever tried to do."

"I've never had anything to do with the business before. You all made damn sure of that. So, what does that have to do with me now?"

"Because when it all comes down to it, now I know that you don't have my back."

"Cam, I have literally had your back since the day you were born. So, what if you don't work for the business anymore? Neither does dad. There is plenty enough money. That will be the least of your worries. You may be a single man now, but maybe that's what you need until you can learn how to love a woman properly," Jada said. "At the end of the day, you have regained your freedom, and you have my husband to thank for that. You got some damn nerve talking all this shit about him after all that he's done for you."

"That nigga don't give a fuck about me. He did that shit because you're his wife," I said. "You asked what this has to do with you? You are literally sleeping with the enemy."

"The enemy? Wow," Jada shook her head in disbelief. "Today was supposed to be a happy, celebratory day, but you had to start with the bullshit. I don't have time for this shit. When you get yourself together and realize that I'm still your sister, give me a call. I'm out."

I shrugged my shoulders and watched as my sister went back into the house.

JADA

"So ... the rehearsal and rehearsal dinner were a success just like the joint bachelor-bachelorette party we surprised them with," Malik said, rubbing his hands together.

I nodded with a smile as I gathered a couple of empty plates and arranged them into a neat stack. The rehearsal dinner for Vanessa and DJ had ended nearly an hour earlier and the venue was empty except for the cleanup staff, Malik, and me.

"Yes. It was very nice. I can tell everyone had a good time."

Malik nodded, walking across the room to where I stood. "We make a hell of a team, you and me."

I shrugged my shoulders but maintained the polite smile on my face. "We did well."

I turned back towards the table in front of me, grabbing a few more plates to stack. Malik shook his head with another smile on his face as he took the plates from my hand and sat them to the side.

"There's a whole group of people getting paid to handle that," he said. "Besides ... don't you have some night before the wedding party with Vanessa and the girls?"

I turned to face him. "Actually no. She said last weekend was more than enough partying for her. So, we're calling it a night, especially since we have to be up early in the morning. Hair, makeup, pictures, brunch, the whole nine," I answered. "I'm turning in after I leave here. I can't show up in the morning with bags under my eyes. Don't want to ruin her perfect pictures because I look a mess."

"Impossible. You could never look a mess," Malik said with a wink as he took a step closer to me.

I hesitated, unsure of how or whether to respond. Malik had been flirting with me since the day Vanessa and DJ settled on the wedding venue. With the present and ever-growing tension in my marriage, I had welcomed the attention. Malik was very well aware of the fact that I was married and who I was married to. I figured his advances were harmless. However, we had history and I wanted to make sure that I did not lead him on to believe that our innocent flirty interactions were anything more than that.

"Thank you," I said. "Don't you have a party to get to with DJ?"

I turned away from Malik and reached for my purse. I sat the Gucci shoulder bag on the table and began to dig around for my keys.

"I do," Malik said. He paused, reaching for my hand and pulling me back towards him. When he wrapped his arms around my waist, my body froze in his embrace. "However, I'd be more than happy to skip DJ's party … if you gave me a reason. I know your place isn't too far from here."

Again, my body froze – this time at Malik's suggestion. Apparently, I had allowed what I thought was harmless flirting to go a step too far. Before I could pull away, Malik ran his fingers through my hair, caressed the side of my face, and pressed his lips against mine. He must have interpreted my lack of resistance as a green light for him to continue his pursuit. For a brief moment, my body relaxed in his arms, reminiscing over the familiarity of his touch.

But then I came to my senses.

I pulled away from him – removing my lips from his although he kept his hands on my hips.

"Malik, I'm married."

"I know."

"And my husband … do you know who he is?"

Malik sighed. He removed his hands from my body, dropping them at his sides. "Yeah, I know. I'm playing with fire right now."

"Literally."

Malik laughed. "You're right. I just …" He hesitated, releasing another sigh. "I feel like I missed my chance with you. I feel like I ended things prematurely and maybe if I hadn't …"

I shook my head. "We can't dwell on the 'what ifs' and hypothetical situations. We had our moment, but it is what it is. I believe that things happen for a reason. Everything worked out the way it was supposed to."

Malik shrugged his shoulders.

"Yeah I guess," he said with a laugh. "Can't blame a guy for trying."

"Maybe I can't, but I'm pretty sure Aaron would."

Malik laughed again, this time taking a step away from me and raising his hands defensively. "Can I at least walk you to your car?"

I nodded. "I suppose there's no harm in that."

I grabbed the rest of my things and Malik followed me outside where Danny was waiting for me at the Escalade. Danny hopped out of the truck and greeted us before opening the rear door and returning to the driver's seat. I climbed into the vehicle while Malik stood at the door with his hand resting on the handle.

"I apologize if I made things a little awkward," he said.

I cut my eyes towards Danny, who appeared to be oblivious to Malik and our conversation. Although Danny was responsible for protecting me, I knew that he ultimately worked for my husband. I trusted Danny with my life, but I put nothing past anyone. I didn't want anything about this evening to be reported back to Aaron.

"No need for an apology," I responded, eager to end the conversation. "I completely understand. It's fine."

"Cool. I just wanted to make sure that I didn't make you too uncomfortable," he said. "Don't want to add any stress or tension to the day tomorrow."

I shook my head with a forced, friendly smile. "It's fine," I repeated. "Tomorrow will run smoothly. We're going to get our best friends down the aisle, and everything will be fine."

Malik nodded in acknowledgment. "Good night, Jada."

"Good night."

Malik closed the door, and I buckled my seat belt.

After starting the engine, Danny asked, "Where to, Mrs. Mercer?"

"The condo, please."

Staying at the condo would put me much closer to the wedding venue in the morning. It would allow me to sleep in a little bit longer before the long, big day that laid ahead of us. After Danny dropped me off, I made my way up the elevator. When I unlocked my door, I expected to walk into a quiet, dark place. However, I was surprised by lights on throughout the living area and the sounds of the television coming from the bedroom.

After the shooting, the locks were changed and upgraded. Aaron and my father were the only ones with keys. I dropped my purse on the kitchen island and headed back to my room. I reached the doorway, leaning against the frame to kick off my heels. Aaron sat on the bench at the foot of the bed watching ESPN. He turned towards me with a smile.

"Hi."

"Hi," I greeted him, not hiding my surprise from my voice. "I thought you weren't going to be able to make it this weekend."

Aaron shrugged his shoulders. "Plans changed. I had some business on the west coast, but Luke took care of it for me. I went to the house to surprise you, but you weren't there. I figured you'd show up here since the wedding venue is downtown," he said. He extended his hand towards me. "Come here."

I crossed the room, standing in front of him. He hugged my waist before I bent down to kiss his lips. I sat down next to him on the bench, and Aaron reached for the remote, turning down the volume before he continued to speak.

"How was your day?"

I shrugged my shoulders. I'm sure he wasn't interested in all the boring details of wedding planning and there was no way in hell I was going to tell him about what happened with Malik. "Busy with wedding stuff. I'm just getting back from the rehearsal dinner. Tomorrow is going to be a production," I answered with a laugh. "How was your day?"

Aaron sighed heavily. "That's actually part of the reason that I'm here," he answered. "We need to talk."

"Talk? About what?"

"My dad is back in the hospital."

"Oh no! Is he okay? What happened?"

I reached for Aaron's hand, holding it tightly.

"He's had a setback dealing with the treatment," he answered. "He's kind of down right now."

"Damn, baby. I'm happy to see you, but shouldn't you be down there with him right now?"

"He's stable at the moment, but we need to talk about what this means for us."

My face wrinkled into a confused frown. "What do you mean?"

"We need to talk about what this means for our family and the near future, mama."

I pulled my hand away from his. I fought hard not to release a sigh, but it was late, and I did not want to spend my night talking about the future.

"Baby, I'm sorry to hear that your dad is in the hospital, but do we have to do this tonight?" I asked him.

"I know you have a busy weekend, but I'm not going to be in town that long. We need to have this conversation in person, mama. There are some changes on the way that you need to know about," he said.

I stood up from the bench, shaking my head.

"Then let's talk tomorrow night or Sunday."

"Mama, I –."

"Aaron, please."

Aaron sighed, rubbing his hands over his face. When he stood up from the bench, I noticed the tired look in his eyes. For a split second, I thought about reconsidering my request to push the conversation. However, I was tired too.

"Alright, Jada. Forget it. We'll talk another day."

Aaron turned the television and the lights off. I stood by the bench and watched as he walked to his side of the bed, stripped down to his underwear and climbed under the covers. I shook my head before heading in the bathroom. After washing my makeup off and preparing for bed, I returned to our room and got under the covers next to Aaron. He laid on his back in the darkness with his eyes closed. I scooted closer to him, draping my leg over his and resting my head on his chest. He seemed dejected when I asked him to push whatever he wanted to discuss. Even though I didn't feel like talking, I knew there was one way I could take his mind off of his troubles. My hand drifted down to his abdomen, my fingers tracing the outlines of the muscles. He didn't respond or react, so I kept going and slipped my hand inside his underwear. Without opening his eyes, Aaron grabbed my hand, pulling it up to his mouth where he kissed it softly.

"You've got a long day tomorrow," he said. "Good night."

I looked on in disbelief while I watched Aaron turn his back towards me as he shifted onto his side. I knew he probably wasn't happy about me brushing off his conversation when he flew in town to be with me – especially while his father was in the hospital. Still, Aaron had never rejected my sexual advances. I truly didn't know how to respond.

All I could do was say, "Goodnight," and turn on my side as well. Closing my eyes, I willed myself to fall asleep quickly.

AARON

Vanessa and DJ's wedding ceremony was beautiful. Extravagance was everywhere, even down to the smallest details. Jada was right. The wedding was definitely a production – a big elaborate show. While sitting in the audience I couldn't help but wonder if this was the type of ceremony Jada wanted. So much had happened since she agreed to our courthouse wedding that I was starting to wonder if we would ever have our formal ceremony. Sitting at my table during the reception, I sipped my drink and watched the crowd. I did not know the majority of the people in the room. It was not my scene at all. I was truly just there to support my wife and her best friend. As my eyes continued to scan the room, they eventually rested on Jada and Malik standing near the bar with some members of the bridal party. Although they were standing with a group, Jada and Malik appeared to be having their own conversation.

Something about the look in his eyes while he smiled in her face caused my jaw to tighten. I shook my head and took another sip of my drink. I had never been the jealous type. I didn't know why I was allowing that clown to get under my skin. I was aware that the two had history, but Jada was my wife.

She was carrying my last name. She had never given me the feeling that she would ever betray our bond. As far as I was concerned, Malik didn't stand a chance in hell with her. Still, I did not particularly care for the way that he was standing so close to her and occasionally touching her elbow while they carried on their conversation. I drained the rest of my glass and then stood up from my seat.

Crossing the room, I made my way to my wife right as the DJ started to play a slow song. With my hand on Jada's waist, I looked at Malik and said, "Mind if I steal her away for a dance?"

Malik smirked but took a step back. "Nah, man. You got it."

Jada excused herself from their conversation while I led her to the dance floor. With one hand on the small of her back, I used my other hand to hold hers as we began to sway to the music. I stared at her with a look of admiration in my eyes. Vanessa had been a beautiful bride, but my wife's beauty was unmatched. Her hair and makeup were styled to perfection and only added to the overall appeal from the dress that complimented her frame.

"You look absolutely amazing tonight," I said into her ear before kissing her on the cheek.

"Thank you," she said with a smile. Rubbing my shoulder, she said, "You clean up pretty well yourself, Mr. Mercer."

We danced for a few more moments with silence between us.

"Thank you again for coming to the wedding. You've been so busy with work and now your dad is in the hospital. I just really appreciate you being up here this weekend," she said. "I know you can't stay long, but how long will you be here?"

"The rest of the weekend. I'm flying back on Monday afternoon."

"So, you're going to the house tonight?"

I frowned. "Yes. Will you be there?"

Jada sighed. She knew I was still frustrated that she had not sold the condo. We were both shot there. I killed Mikey Pitt there. For the life of me I couldn't understand why she was holding on to that place.

"Yes. If you are going to be at the house, so will I. I know you wanted to talk tonight, so we can talk. Hopefully, it's nothing too heavy," she said. "Since you took time out of your busy schedule to be here with me, I would like to have a relaxing weekend with my husband. Hopefully that's not too much to ask."

"Of course not," I answered her.

I pulled her body closer to mine and she relaxed, resting her head against my chest. After the song was over, we made our way back to our table, where we made it through the rest of the evening sharing small talk and a few laughs. Soon it was time to send off the new bride and groom and the guests started to clear out shortly thereafter. After checking in with the wedding planner and their team to make sure everything was taken care of, Jada made her way through the crowd to me.

"I just need to finish grabbing my things and then I'm getting out of here," she said. "See you at home?"

"See you at home."

Jada kissed me on the lips before turning and disappearing into the crowd again. I stepped out of the venue into the brisk, night air and made my way to my Aston Martin. I quickly made my way to the house to relieve the nanny. AJ was already sleeping peacefully. After a nice hot shower, I pulled on some clothes and made my way into the bedroom. Jada arrived home a short while later. She had already changed into more comfortable clothing and washed the makeup from her face. Her hair was still styled in the long, slicked back ponytail from the wedding. She kicked off her sandals and climbed into the bed next to me. She laid her head on my chest.

"So, what did you want to talk about?"

I hesitated, but I knew exactly what I needed to tell her. This conversation was long overdue. I could have tried to ease my way into it, but what good would that have done? The sooner I got to the point, the sooner we could get it over with.

"We need to move to Miami. Full time," I said.

Jada raised her head from my chest and looked at me with questioning eyes.

"What?"

"My father isn't getting any better. I've been filling in for him on an interim basis, but it will be made official shortly. When that happens, I will need to be in Miami full time, and if that's where I am going to need to be, you and the kids will need to be there also."

"What do you mean by full-time?"

"I mean that I'm selling this house. I'm meeting with my real estate agent Monday before my flight leaves."

Jada sat up in the bed completely, leaning against the headboard and looking straight ahead. She pulled her knees up to her chest, shaking her head before she spoke again.

"I suppose this is one of those hard decisions you make for our family, huh? One of those things where I'm just supposed to accept what you say and fall in line?"

"Jada, you knew from day one that my life was based in Miami. In the back of your mind, you had to know that I would need to go back when my business was finished in Atlanta. That day has come. Your dad is officially retired, Cameron is out of prison, and PO is on the way to smoothing things out with the mayor," I told her. "I've told you before that my job as your husband is to love, provide for, and to protect you. I can't protect you to the best of my ability if we're maintaining residences in two different states. With everything I have on my plate, I don't need to be worrying about your safety as well. The house that's being built – our house – is almost complete. It's time that we are all under the same roof in Miami."

Jada pushed the covers back and got out of the bed. She paced the floor for a moment before stopping to look at me.

"No," she said.

I frowned. "No? What do you mean, no?"

"No," she repeated herself. "You can't just spring something like this on me and tell me you're selling the house and expect that to be it."

"I'm not springing anything on you," I countered. "Jada, I've been trying to have this conversation for months. I've been trying to talk to you, but all you want to do is take your clothes off so you can temporarily avoid any real conversation. That doesn't solve anything, mama. All it does is provide a distraction from our issues."

Jada smirked and shook her head. "You're the only man I've ever known that called sex with his wife a distraction."

"You know what I mean. Nothing is ever going to get settled if we can't finish a serious conversation."

"It was worth a shot," she mumbled.

She stood at the side of our bed with her hands on her hips. I looked at her expectantly. I expected her to acknowledge that everything I said was logical. It only made sense in my mind that we move to Miami. I couldn't understand how she did not see that.

"Aaron, you can't just pop back up from the dead and demand that I move my entire life to Miami. You are taking over for your father, and I understand that. I understand that you love us and want to protect us, but when you were gone AJ and I were just fine," she said. "My family, my friends, my businesses ... everything is in Atlanta. Things are still strained between me and my brother and father and you want me to just walk away from my whole life because I took your last name?"

I let out a heavy sigh and got out of the bed as well. I walked over to where she stood, taking her hands in mine.

"No one is asking you to walk away from your whole life.

I'm asking you to commit to the life you signed up for when you agreed to be my wife. AJ, Olivia, me … we're your family now too. You can still handle business from Miami. I would expect that you would need to occasionally fly back and forth to Atlanta, but our life needs to be in Miami now," I told her. "Yes, things are still strained between you and your father, but he will understand that you need to relocate to be with your husband. That shit with Cameron … you're gonna have to let that go, mama. I've done more for him than I would have if he was anybody else. I paid for his legal team and orchestrated the events behind the scenes that ultimately allowed him to regain his freedom. If he still has an issue with me, that's his problem. He made his bed, and he needs to lie in it. You can't fix that shit."

Jada pulled her hands away from mine, but she didn't move her body.

"Look, I'm going to move forward with putting the house on the market and our family will be in Miami sooner rather than later," I said to her. "The quicker you get on board with that the smoother this will all go."

Jada glared at me with her hands resting at her sides. I caressed the side of her face before cupping her chin and kissing her on the lips.

"Come back to bed," I told her. "You had a long day, and I'm tired. We can continue this conversation in the morning if you feel the need to do so."

I walked back to my side of the bed, turned off the lamp on my bedside table, and climbed under the covers. Jada hesitated but then got back into the bed as well.

I kissed her on the cheek. "Goodnight."

Jada turned away from me without responding. I shook my head and closed my eyes. She would get over her attitude. She always did.

PO

"...*A*nd don't forget we have the parent-teacher conference with the twins' Science teacher tomorrow," Kiara said from the doorway of our bedroom.

"I got you."

"Cool," she said. "Are you going to be back for dinner tonight?"

I sat on the edge of the bed to put on my shoes. I shrugged my shoulders while she looked at me expectantly.

"Okay. Well, just let me know when you're on your way back."

"Will do," I said, kissing her on the cheek.

I headed out of the house and hopped into my truck. I started the engine and dialed Zo's number before pulling off.

"Boss man. What's up?"

"Do you have eyes on him?"

"Yeah, I do. He's at his crib right now," Zo answered. "Are you sure you don't want me to take care of him. I could get rid of his ass before you could even get to the highway."

"Yeah I'm sure. I'll be over there as soon as I can."

I ended the call and started the drive. When Prime started

working for us, he had shown much promise and generated even more profit. It was a shame that he had wasted our time and ultimately his life. I had given him more than enough rope to hang himself. From messing with the money, to trying to set his own rules, to going behind my back to work with the guys from New York, his time had come. I would not afford him another day to disrespect my position.

It took less than fifteen minutes for me to get to Prime's neighborhood. I parked a couple of houses down the block. Before getting out of the car, I made sure to conceal my gun. I exited my truck and started to walk towards his house, pausing along the way when I reached Zo's car. I tapped on his window.

"Let's go."

Zo quickly got out of his vehicle and walked alongside of me. When we reached the front door, I knocked loudly. While waiting for Prime to answer the door, I turned towards Zo.

"Did you already reach out to JB?"

"Yep, and he's just waiting on my call."

"Good."

A few moments later Prime answered the door with a surprised look on his face and a lit blunt between his fingers.

"Come in."

He stepped to the side allowing Zo and I to enter before closing the front door.

"An unannounced visit from the boss man and his right hand," Prime said, raising the blunt to his lips. "What's this about?"

"Let's walk and talk," I answered.

Familiar with the layout of his house, I walked further into the residence until I reached the door that lead down to the basement. I opened the door and started down the steps. I heard Prime hesitate before he followed me down the steps. Zo was right behind him. When I got to the basement, I stopped at the two sofas that sat opposite one another. Prime took a seat on one of the sofas, motioning for us to have a seat as well.

"I suppose I already know why you're here," he said. "You might as well have a seat."

I shook my head. "If you know why we're here, you should know that I won't be staying long."

Prime smirked and shook his head. "So, what finally did it, huh? The shit with the money?" he asked. "Or was it the new guys? You found out I was messing with the New York niggas you and Julian shut down?"

Zo frowned. "Nigga, does it even matter?"

"I guess not," Prime answered.

"You should realize you were lucky enough to last this long," Zo told him. "If it were up to me, your ass would have been gone months ago."

And he was right. I should have taken care of Prime a while ago. I was so focused on the transition and making nice with the mayor that I slipped on taking care of my business. If I had handled my business like normal, Prime would have been gone weeks ago. I pulled my gun out, watching Prime while I attached the silencer. Prime closed his eyes and relaxed, leaning back against the sofa and raising the blunt to his lips again. Without hesitation, I raised my weapon firing one fatal bullet through his temple. I lowered my gun by my side and turned towards Zo.

"So you already have his replacement lined up?"

Zo nodded. "Nick. He's ready, willing, and able."

"Nick? Your brother, Nick?"

"Yep. Trust me, Boss. I don't play favorites," Zo answered. "I wouldn't put him out there if he wasn't truly ready."

"Alright then. Works for me," I said.

I handed him the gun.

"Get rid of this, and go on and call JB. Make sure they wipe this place down," I instructed him. "You and I were never here."

"Consider it done," Zo agreed.

I headed for the stairs and exited the house. I made my way to my truck and slid into the passenger seat. Before pulling off, I sent a text message.

"It's done."

Mayor Richardson sent a reply text thanking me for handling our mutual issue. I didn't respond. Instead, I called Kiara and let her know that I had one more stop before I headed back home.

JADA

Children birthday parties had never been my scene. However, things change as you grow older and have a family of your own. I stood in the backyard of my father's home watching the party guests enjoy AJ's animal safari themed first birthday party. After opening gifts and eating cake, the party was starting to wind down, but everyone still appeared to be having a good time. In my opinion, the party was way over the top, especially for a one-year-old, but I was learning that Aaron spared no expense when it came to his loved ones. There was a second party planned in Miami for the following weekend.

My attention shifted when I noticed Olivia jogging towards me with AJ on her hip. My niece Katy was right behind them.

"This is the best party ever!" Katy shouted.

Olivia nodded and smiled. "Yeah, I'm having a lot of fun," she said. "This is really cool."

"I'm glad you girls are having fun," I said with a smile of my own. "Livvy, do you want me to take the baby?"

Olivia shook her head. "No. It's fine. We're going to look at some more animals."

I watched as the kids took off. A few moments later, Aaron appeared by my side.

"Hey mama," he said, kissing me on the cheek.

"Hey ... you getting ready to leave?"

Aaron sighed. "Unfortunately. I have to be at the airport in a little bit."

"It's okay. The party's almost over anyway," I said. I laughed and shook my head. "This shit was so over the top."

Aaron smiled and wrapped an arm around my shoulders, pulling me closer to him. "If you think this is something just wait until you see what Sophia Mercer has planned for next week."

I laughed a little harder. "I'm almost scared to. If it tops this, I can't even imagine," I said.

"Just prepare yourself," Aaron said as he looked down at his watch.

"You gotta go?"

Aaron nodded. "Yeah, mama. I gotta go," he said. "Kiss my babies for me. See you in Miami."

Aaron kissed me on the lips before leaving. After watching the kids and party guests for a few more minutes I decided I needed a drink. I headed inside of the house. On my way to the kitchen I passed Cameron, who was laughing and talking with a family friend. He cut his eyes towards me but then turned away, refusing to speak. I shook my head and rolled my eyes as they continued on to the backyard. Cameron had not spoken to me in weeks. When I reached the kitchen, I went in search of a bottle of wine and a glass. Moments later, Vanessa entered the kitchen with a large, wrapped box in her hands.

"Hey lady!" she greeted me with a warm smile.

"Well hello Mrs. Jones," I said, taking a sip from my glass. "I wasn't expecting to see you today. I thought you didn't get back from your honeymoon until tomorrow."

Vanessa shook her head. "Nope. We got back in late last night. DJ has to head out tomorrow for some tour or something," she said. "You know he's always got something going on with work."

"Sounds familiar," I mumbled.

Vanessa frowned momentarily but then said, "Speaking of husbands, I saw yours driving away when I pulled into the neighborhood."

"What can I say?" I laughed. "He's always got something going on with work."

"I know how you feel, sister." Changing the subject, Vanessa said, "But wine at a kid's birthday party?"

I shrugged my shoulders. "It has been a day. This party has been over the top to say the least."

"I bet. I was surprised to see that you had the party here. I figured it would have been more convenient to have the party at your house."

Raising my glass to my lips I said, "Not when my house won't be my house for much longer."

"What?"

I sat my glass down and turned towards my best friend.

"Aaron's selling the house. He's working with his real estate agent to put it on the market and prepare for showings."

"What? I know I've been busy the past few weeks with wedding things, but when the hell did that happen?"

"He told me last week."

"Told you?"

"Yes. Told me."

Vanessa frowned in confusion. "But why? I love your condo, but it's a shoebox compared to the house in Sandy Springs," she said. "If you get rid of the house, where are you all going to live?"

"Miami."

"What?" Vanessa asked.

I shrugged my shoulders.

"Now I'm the one that needs a glass of wine," Vanessa said.

After grabbing and filling her own glass, she sat down on a stool next to me.

"So he came up here last weekend for the wedding and just tells you that he's selling the house and you're moving to Miami. Just like that?"

"Just like that," I answered. "He said I can keep the condo so I have a place to stay when I'm up here for work or visiting family and friends. I suppose that's a compromise on his part. He wanted me to get rid of the condo at first."

"But Julian bought it for you when we graduated college."

"I know," I said, "but he wanted me to get a place with better security. A place where we didn't both get shot."

Vanessa smirked. "A place that Malik and Israel don't know about."

"Yeah that too."

"How do you feel about that?" Vanessa asked with a look of concern on her face.

"Does it even matter?" I asked, shrugging my shoulders.

"Of course it does."

"You're probably the only person that cares," I said, taking another long sip from my wine glass.

"I'm asking as your best friend. You've been through a lot these last couple of years, Jay. Of course I want to know how you're doing and how you feel about all of this," she said. "Your whole life is in Atlanta. Moving to Miami is a big deal."

"Yeah it is, but there's not much I can do about it. I put up resistance initially, but that didn't change anything. Aaron's father isn't doing too well. He'll be taking over for him soon, and the house he was having built in Miami is almost finished. He wants me, him, and the kids all under the same roof. It's a done deal," I said. "We'll be in Miami before the end of the summer."

"Wow."

"Yeah. Wow," I said. "I don't know, Ness. It's just a lot. Voicing my opposition at this point doesn't matter, and I just …

I don't know. I guess I didn't realize that this was going to be my life."

Vanessa frowned again. "What do you mean?"

"I mean that I've always been the strong independent woman that handled her own business and did as she pleased. My father's lifestyle afforded me certain luxuries, but it's not like I've been a kept woman sitting on my ass and spending other people's money. I wanted to work. I needed to work, and running my businesses give me a personal satisfaction. In the beginning, Aaron loved that I had some business about myself … at least I thought he did," I said. "Now all of that seems to have changed. I'm not even allowed to have input on where I lay my head at night. I've never been the type to shut up and go along to get along. I'm not sure if I can. I've always been able to have a voice in my relationships. Hell, the whole time I was with Israel I always felt that I had the freedom to make certain decisions about my personal and professional life."

"Jada, you can't compare the two."

"I'm not. I promise that's not what I'm trying to do," I said. "They are not the same. I love Aaron. I love him more than I've loved anybody. I don't want to live my life without him. When I thought that I would have to, that shit almost broke me. I want to be with him, but all of this feels eerily similar to the life my mother had. Even still … I want to be his wife. I just don't know if I can be the type of wife that he needs in order for us to both be happy."

"Damn, Jada. Have you told him this?"

I shook my head.

"I don't know what good that's going to do right now. There are still feelings and thoughts in my head that I need to sort out before I even approach him. All the reasons he listed for the move to Miami are logical. He's about to be in charge of the whole operation. He won't have time to split between Atlanta when his focus needs to be on other things. I can easily fly back and forth to check on things at the restaurant and the boutique, and Ayanna is holding things down at the salon. I want the kids to be together with their father. I just don't know why I can't just suck it up and go with the flow," I said. Shrugging my shoulders, I said, "Maybe I'm the problem, but this situation is exactly why I was upset when I found out who he was. I'm not sure I ever wanted this life, but I don't think I can live without him."

"You're not going to be able to get on the same page if you two don't talk about it," Vanessa said. "If you want to fix things, instead of just going with the flow, you're going to have to talk to him."

"I will. After I gather my thoughts," I said. I downed the rest of my wine and said, "But right now, I need to wrap this party up."

"Jada, I think –"

"Everything else can wait," I said. "Come on outside with me."

Vanessa sighed and hesitated before downing the rest of her glass and following me to the backyard.

PO

unny how so much could change in such a small amount of time, I thought as I continued my drive. I was in route to Ruth Chris Steakhouse to meet the mayor for lunch. We had a number of things to discuss about the recent changes. After taking over for Julian at the beginning of the year, I was finally starting to feel settled. I was starting to feel at ease with the shift in power and the way that things were operating under my control. Zo's brother, Nick, had taken over Prime's territory and exceeded my expectations as his replacement. With more growth and more income than anticipated, I was working with Tony to find new ways to clean our money.

With the recent increase in the pace of the business, I was struggling to balance family time. Aisha graduated high school a few weeks prior. I had almost missed the ceremony dealing with a work-related issue. I was not able to spend as much time with my girls as I would have liked, but Kiara was doing a great job of holding things down around the house. I hoped to have more family time once my team and I adjusted to the new pace of business.

Julian was enjoying his retirement while Cameron was

begrudgingly trying to redefine his life on the outside of the business his family had been so instrumental in growing. Luke had not been back to Atlanta since Cameron's release, and Aaron was seemingly transitioning his life back to Miami. I was finally alone at the helm. During the transition and subsequent changes, Zo proved why he was the logical choice to be my right-hand man. We made a great team. Aside from the issues Prime brought about, I was expanding the business and keeping things quiet – just how the mayor liked.

After leaving my vehicle with the valet, I entered the restaurant and informed the hostess of the name for our party. To my surprise, she led me to a private dining room. I didn't understand the need for such secrecy for a quick lunch meeting. When we reached the room, Mayor Richardson was at a table set for three people sipping a glass of water. The hostess left us alone.

"PO, good to see you," the mayor said, standing to shake my hand.

I sat down after greeting him.

"What's going on?" I asked.

Mayor Richardson shrugged his shoulders casually with a pleasant smile on his face. "Just a meeting of the minds."

I smiled and nodded in acknowledgment. Things had started to become much more amicable between the mayor and myself, but sometimes I still found him annoying. He carried on as if he was always on the campaign trail. I rarely got a direct answer from him.

"You've had an incredible couple of months. It seems like things are just getting better, especially now that you've handled that unfortunate little problem you had," the mayor stated, referencing Prime. "In all honesty, I'm excited to hear about your updates. When you win, we all win. I know I for one definitely enjoy the extra padding to my pockets."

I let out a slight laugh, nodding again. I'm sure he did appreciate the extra padding, because it had definitely increased in the last few months or so. My financial obligation with the mayor was not a flat fee. Instead, our arrangement was more of a percentage of profits – the more money I made meant more money for him and vice versa.

"I'm definitely winning right now," I agreed with the mayor. "However, making more money means I need to find new avenues to make it clean."

"I can help with that," Mayor Richardson stated. "I have several connections with small business owners on the west side of town that may be looking for investors. I'm also in good with several property managers in need of new tenants if you want to open your own store or business of some sort. Just let me know what you need, and I'm sure I can help make it happen."

"I appreciate that. I've been going over some ideas with one of my lawyers, so I should have a plan pretty soon."

"Good. I want to be of assistance in any way I can so we can keep business moving forward in such a positive direction."

Mayor Richardson paused to take a sip of his water.

"I'm sure you're probably wondering why I opted for private dining today and who is the other lunch guest …"

I shrugged my shoulders.

"Since you and I are on the same page now and business is running smoothly I figured it was time that we all sat down together – you, me … and Chief Stroud," Mayor Richardson stated. "With this being a pretty popular lunch spot, I figured it would be best if the three of us dined in privacy."

The mayor had a good point, and I agreed with him. The mayor and the police chief were sure to draw attention by themselves. The last thing anyone needed was for questions to start being asked, such as why the two of them were having lunch with me. Julian Reid was different. Along the way to the top of a criminal empire, he also built a reputation around the city as a business owner and philanthropist. I had not done either. In all my time at Julian's right side, all I ever cared about was the money. Therefore, I absolutely had to agree with the mayor that the three of us dining in public would be a lot different than Julian breaking bread with the mayor and chief of the Atlanta police department.

Mayor Richardson glanced at his cell phone before addressing me again. "Chief will be here shortly. He's already on the way," he said. "In the meantime, I'll have the waitress bring a bottle of champagne. I wasn't sure what to think of you in the beginning, PO. You have made me a believer of the potential Julian Reid saw in you. Order has been restored, and I am confident that you will keep things running smoothly for a long time to come. I feel that and our budding business relationship is worthy of a toast."

"I'll certainly drink to that."

JADA

Yawning, I stretched my arms and felt more rested than I had in a very long time. I opened my eyes but frowned at the darkness of the room. Knowing that it had to be well into the morning, I sat up and reached for my phone. It was almost noon. I looked up to see that the room darkening curtains had been drawn, eliminating any light into the room. I quickly got up from the bed, reaching for my robe to cover the short, silk nightgown I wore. I was sliding my feet into my slippers when I heard the bedroom door open.

"Look, mommy's awake," I heard Aaron say.

I turned around and instantly smiled when I saw Aaron walking towards me with AJ in his arms. The two were already dressed for the day while I had barely wiped the sleep out of my eyes.

"Good morning," Aaron said, kissing me on the cheek.

"Morning. How long have you been up?"

Aaron shrugged his shoulders and sat down on the edge of the bed. "A couple of hours. You seemed like you could use some more rest, so I closed the curtains and let you sleep. I figured a few more hours couldn't hurt … especially after last night."

He winked at me, and I laughed.

"You were right. It definitely helped. I feel more rested than I have in a while," I said. "I just didn't plan on sleeping in this long."

"You have plans for the day?"

I shrugged my shoulders. "Nothing major. Dani invited me to go shopping. I was going to see if your mom or Rosa could watch the baby if you have to work."

Aaron smiled.

"You're getting out of the house?"

"I *need* to get out of the house," I responded. "Besides the few places I've been with you, I feel like I've been holed up in here. Your parents' place is lovely baby, but I need to see more of the city."

I had been in Miami since AJ's birthday party three weeks prior. I originally planned to be in Miami for a week. However, Aaron received a cash offer on the house, and he had people packing and clearing out our things. With the plan for our family to transition to Miami drawing closer, Aaron asked that I spend some additional time in Miami to get a good feel for what our lives would be like once I officially moved. I had not done a good job of exploring my surroundings.

"I understand, and I'm sure Mom or Rosa will be more than happy to watch this little guy so you can get out," he said. "Dani has her own security, but I can ask Julio to tag along if you would like."

I shook my head while taking AJ into my arms. "I don't think that's really necessary."

"Alright," Aaron said standing up. "I'll go speak to my mom. I need to head out to take care of some business, but I'll be back by early evening. Try to be home in time enough for me to take you to dinner around seven. Maybe we can go to that steak place you like on Brickell Ave."

"Sounds good."

"Bet. I'll hit you up later. See you tonight."

Aaron got AJ settled with his mother before leaving the house, which allowed me to get dressed in peace. After getting ready, I found my sister in law, and we departed for the Shops at Merrick Park. We ate lunch before spending hours shopping and an unnecessary amount of money. I enjoyed my time away from the Mercer mansion. There was plenty to keep me entertained at the family estate, but it was nice to have a girl's day out without the kids. It was a distraction from the thoughts that recently occupied my mind. What I had not yet shared with my husband was that even though I agreed to spend the time in Miami, the three weeks I had been in town did nothing to excite me about the move.

I missed Atlanta. I missed going to work. I missed my family and friends. It had only been three weeks. I couldn't imagine how I would feel when I actually lived in Miami full time. In addition, there was the fact that since he took over for his father, I was seeing way less of my husband than I was used to. That was understandable but it still did nothing to make me feel at home in Miami. I wasn't thrilled about the idea of spending the majority of the day without him and going to sleep at night in an empty bed. I felt like I was becoming the very type of woman I told Vanessa I never wanted to be – a kept woman who sat on her hands spending other people's money. Again, I began to question if this was the life that I truly wanted, and if I had known what I was really signing up for when we decided to get married.

Per Aaron's request, Daniella and I returned home in plenty enough time for me to get ready for dinner. I took another shower, styled my hair, and applied my makeup flawlessly before pulling on one of the curve-hugging dresses I purchased from Neiman Marcus. It was seven-thirty when I realized that not only was Aaron not home yet, but he had not made any contact with me throughout the day as he said he would. I sat down on the sofa in the sitting room with my cell phone in my hand. Part of me was understanding of the fact that he was a busy man. Another part of me just wanted to make sure that he was safe. However, there was another part of me – a part that was beyond frustrated that this wasn't the first time I had been stood up for dinner in the three weeks that I had been in Miami.

I dialed his number. There was no response.

Ten minutes later, I texted him. Again, there was no response.

I called him again five minutes after that. Only to be met with voicemail again.

By ten o'clock, I had purchased a red-eye ticket back to Atlanta. I changed from my date night attire to a tank top and a pair of yoga pants. I pulled my hair back into a low ponytail and washed the makeup off my face. After I packed a bag for myself, I headed to AJ's room to pack a bag for him.

"Hey mama," Aaron greeted me as he entered the nursery. I glanced over my shoulder to see that he had a glass of whiskey in his hand. He leaned in and kissed me. The top two buttons on his shirt were undone and the smell of alcohol radiated from him. I could tell this was not his first drink of the night. "I was looking for you."

He paused. I assumed that was when he noticed the small duffel bag I was packing. His face fell into a questioning frown.

"What's going on here?"

I turned around to face him completely and took a deep breath before answering.

"I think I need to go back home for a little bit."

"This is your home, Jada."

"Atlanta ... you know what I mean,"

Aaron shook his head and ran a hand over his face. He took a sip of his drink before speaking to me again.

"So, you were packing up to leave without saying anything to me?"

"I tried to reach you more than once tonight but yeah. I'm saying something now."

Aaron pinched the bridge of his nose. "What's the problem this time?"

"What are you talking about?"

"Jada, it seems like every time something upsets you; you're trying to run away from me or back to Atlanta like this isn't your life now – like Miami isn't your home too," he said. "So, what the fuck did I do this time?"

I frowned.

I didn't appreciate what he was trying to imply. My life was in Atlanta and Miami, and I had been backed into a corner and forced to transition to Miami. I wasn't going to forget about the rest of my family and my businesses because of who I chose to marry.

"Don't do that," I told him. "I'm not about to let you try to play the victim here. Things are strained between us right now. They have been for some time. I need a breather and there's some business I can take care of back ho—in Atlanta."

"You're not going to fix a strained relationship by running away or ignoring it, mama."

Aaron's tone was calm as he looked me directly in my eyes.

"We aren't necessarily spending quality time together trying to work on things either. Things don't really seem to be getting better with me being here," I answered truthfully.

"That's not for my lack of trying," he responded. "I'm sorry about tonight. Something came up with work, and I can't always answer my phone when I'm handling business."

I shrugged my shoulders. "I didn't say that this was your

fault. It just is what it is. Going through the motions isn't help-ing. I just need to clear my head. I need to try to figure some things out."

"Figure out what things?"

Aaron took another sip of his drink, peering at me over the top of the glass.

"Aaron, we can't keep going like this. I can't keep going like this," I told him. "I need to figure out if this is going to work."

He smirked and shook his head. He lowered his glass by his side and stepped away from me to pace the floor. After a few moments passed, he stopped pacing and turned to face me again.

"Jada, I don't get it. I've spent the last several months trying to figure this out, and for the life of me I can't."

I folded my hands in front of me and remained quiet so that he could continue.

"Everything was good between us until the shooting, but we've talked about why I had to go away multiple times. You understand that a move had to be made for your protection until I could take care of Michaela myself. You understand that although it wasn't ideal, I had to handle that situation with Shannon. You know that every decision I've made and every single thing that I do is for you and our family," he said. "I don't make any apologies for who I am, Jada. If anyone should be able to understand that, it should be you. If anyone should be able to deal with this life by my side, it should be you. You were raised by one of the coldest dudes to run the game that I've crossed paths with. You should know what comes along with the terri-tory. I do a pretty good job of providing you with the lifestyle most women dream about, but everything isn't always day parties and Louis Vuitton handbags. It's not always sunshine and rainbows. Tough decisions have to be made and I'm the one doing that now. Those things are falling on me. You are my wife. We are one. What did you expect life to be as Mrs. Mercer?"

I hesitated for a moment. I had to admit the honest truth. I shrugged my shoulders as my eyes watered.

"I don't know," I told him. "Aaron, I love you, but –"

"But you're getting ready to run away again and maybe for good this time," he said, taking another sip of his drink.

"Baby, I –"

He interrupted me, shaking his head. "Just go on and get out of here."

I started to walk towards him. "I just –"

"I said go goddammit!" he shouted. "Leave!"

He threw his glass past my head. My eyes were wide as I heard the shattered pieces of glass fall to the ground. I stopped in my tracks, my hands in front of me defensively.

"Just get the fuck out of here and do whatever you need to do, Jada. There are a million and one things I have to deal with on a daily basis and chasing in behind you as you're constantly running away shouldn't be one of them," he said.

My hands were trembling slightly as I dropped them by my sides and looked down at my feet.

"Fine. My flight leaves in a couple of hours."

Aaron glared at me with his jaw tight. I turned back towards AJ's bag and continued to pack it with clothes and other items.

"Nah. You can go, but you're not taking my son," he said evenly.

I spun back around to face him.

"Our son," I corrected him. "I've already made arrangements –"

Aaron was next to me in a split second, snatching the bag from my hands and throwing it on the floor. "I don't give a fuck," he said. "You want to leave? Fine, but AJ stays here."

I glared at him in disbelief. I thought about challenging him, but the look in his eyes and the shattered glass on the floor urged me to stop. I took a step away from him.

"Whatever, Aaron," I said in a defeated tone.

I headed for the hallway.

Aaron spoke to my back.

"You know … one of these days you're going to realize that you and I are cut from the same cloth. You were built for this life, Jada," he said. "When you stop running from that and realize that we are supposed to be together, I'll be right here waiting on you."

I didn't respond or even turn around to acknowledge him. I headed back to our room to grab my things. After shouldering my bags and grabbing my phone, I headed down the steps to the front door where Julio was already waiting to take me to the airport.

JADA

The salon was busy, even for a Saturday. The sounds of women chatting and gossiping could be heard over the sound of running water and hair dryers. Since we were so busy, I made my way around to drop fresh towels off to the stylist stations and check to see if the nail technicians needed anything. It was only four o'clock in the afternoon, but it had been a long day, and I was looking forward to calling it a day and going home. I spotted Ayanna speaking to the receptionist and headed for the front desk.

"Hey sis," Ayanna greeted me. "I was just going over the remaining appointments for the day. It looks like it's going to be a long one for sure."

I sighed. "It's already been a pretty long one."

"I know, and you don't look like you're feeling too well," Ayanna said. "I got here late today. I'll stay until close. Why don't you head on home?"

"You don't have to tell me twice," I said. "I'm going to finish a few things in my office and then I'm getting out of here. All I want to do is climb in the bed and go to sleep right now."

"I can tell."

"Call me later if –"

I stopped speaking when my attention was drawn to a group of individuals crossing the parking lot headed right for the front door of the salon. Ayanna looked over her shoulder to see what had distracted me. When she noticed Sophia Mercer headed into the salon with her security, Olivia, and AJ, Ayanna turned back towards me with a raised eyebrow.

"Did you know she was in town?"

I shook my head.

No. I had no idea that my mother in law or my kids were in Atlanta. I had not seen them in six weeks. It had been six weeks since the argument where Aaron told me to leave his mother's house, and I had barely spoken to him either. I was taken aback by Sophia's surprise visit to Atlanta, and I am sure that was written all over my face when she walked into the salon.

"Sophia, how are you?" Ayanna greeted her warmly, as the two embraced.

"I am well, darling," she said with a warm smile. "And you?"

"I can't complain at all. I'm excited to see my niece and nephew," Ayanna said. She reached to hug both Olivia and AJ.

Still stunned, I stood motionless with a shocked look still on my face.

Sophia handed AJ to Ayanna and turned towards me with an even wider smile. "Mija, how are you?"

I shrugged my shoulders. "I – I'm fine," I stuttered. "What are you doing here?"

"I thought you might want to see the kids, but also you and I need to chat," she said. She paused and turned towards my sister. "Ayanna, dear, I saw a frozen yogurt place a few doors down. Would you be so kind as to go with Hector and Carlo and take the children for some dessert?"

"No problem," Ayanna said, balancing AJ on her hip. "Let's go kids."

I watched my children head out of the store with my sister

and Sophia's bodyguards close behind. Sophia turned back towards me.

"Is there somewhere more private for you and me to speak?"

"Yeah. Of course," I said. "Follow me."

I led Sophia down the hallway to my office. I closed the door behind her and pulled a chair out for her to sit at my desk.

"I'm sorry I should have asked before we came back here … can I get you anything to drink? Water? Tea?"

Sophia shook her head. "I'm fine. Thank you. Sit. Let's talk."

Instead of walking behind my desk, I sat in the chair next to her. Sophia and I had a good relationship. She accepted me into her family with open arms from day one and was a welcomed maternal figure, especially in the absence of my own mother. She supported my relationship with her only son while being respectful and not overstepping boundaries. During our recent struggles, Sophia never inserted herself in the middle of our business so I was anxious to know the real reason behind her impromptu trip to Atlanta.

"Is everything okay?" I asked. "Are Manny and Aaron alright?"

Sophia smiled as she lovingly squeezed my hand. "Manny is fine, dear. How sweet of you to ask."

"And Aaron?"

Sophia sighed and settled into her chair but still maintained the smile on her face. "Physically … he is alright. However, I must admit that he is the reason for my trip to Atlanta."

I blinked hard fighting to hold in the sigh I wanted to release. Our separation had not brought us any closer to being on the same page. After weeks of strained communication and only seeing my kids on FaceTime, I was wondering if Aaron sent his mother to Atlanta to plead his case for me to come back to Miami.

"Before you ask, no he did not send me here," Sophia stated

as if she were reading my mind. "In fact, he doesn't even know that I'm here."

"What do you mean?"

"He and Lucas are on the west coast handling some business. He won't be back home for a few days," she answered. "I took it upon myself to come visit you. To be quite honest, Aaron would probably be pretty upset if he knew that I was here. He would not be happy with me interceding on his behalf. He's quite like his father that way. They feel they need to handle everything themselves. How dare I offer my assistance?"

Sophia shook her head and released a short laugh. She looked me directly in my eyes.

"He's been carrying on like a moody little child without you, you know?"

I hesitated before respond. "I wouldn't know," I told her. "We've barely spoken. There's just too much tension between us right now."

"Jada, you haven't seen your husband or kids in over a month," she said. "What sort of tension could be keeping you away from your family for so long?"

I inhaled sharply, shaking my head while I looked down at my hands. I shrugged my shoulders again.

"Things have seemed a bit … off since he got rid of Michaela Pitt," Sophia said, "but am I correct in assuming that the recent disconnect is related to your move to Miami?"

I nodded.

Sophia sighed and rubbed my cheek before speaking again. "I figured that may be the reason," she stated. "Mija, do you know who you are married to?"

"Yes, but –"

"My sweet girl, that's the problem. There is no 'but'. Your husband is the head of the Cartel. There are things that must be done for the sake of the business regardless of our personal feelings," she said. "Trust me. I know how you must feel."

I raised an eyebrow.

"My son has so much of his father in him, and I can see a lot of myself in you. There are so many similarities, my dear. You feel like you're walking away from your family, your friends, and the only life you've ever known," she said. "You feel that so much of who you are is tied to this city, and you probably can't begin to comprehend what your life is going to look like in Miami."

I nodded again. Sophia's words were spot on.

"Jada, I know you probably are taking issue with the fact that this decision was made for you. Again, I know how you feel," Sophia said. "I was younger than you are now when I fell in love with Manny. He proved himself to my father and took over the business when we were still very young. Although he was eager to succeed my father, there was one thing he was very adamant about. He demanded to run the business from Miami, and my father agreed. That was a decision made without any consideration for what I wanted. With little notice, I moved my entire life to Miami for the man that I loved – the man that was responsible for my heart and well-being but also a multi mullion dollar business."

Sophia squeezed my hand again as she continued to speak to me.

"I was a young mother not only in a new city, but a new country, that I was very unfamiliar with. I struggled with the change and getting used to my new surroundings. It took some time for me to get used to living in America and not always getting my way," she said with a smile. "I am the only daughter of Alejandro Ramirez. I was very used to getting my way. My whole world changed overnight, and I initially struggled with the shift. However, I held on strong to my reason why. When I no longer felt like an equal partner in my relationship and a spectator to my own life, I had to remember why I was there. I had to remember what made me stay. I love Manny more than I ever knew was humanly possible, and deep in my heart I know he's always felt the same way about me. I had to trust that even when decisions were made for me that they were always for my best interest. I had to trust that he would never steer me wrong and never let me down, and for almost forty years, he has never failed me. This beautiful life that I have I owe to him, and I know that I would have made a terrible mistake if I had left him when we were younger."

Sophia held on to both of my hands.

"Jada, my son loves you. He loves you probably more than he ever knew was humanly possible," she said with a smile. "His eyes light up whenever you enter the room or your name crosses his lips. He is so much like his father – sometimes to his detriment. I know you feel like a fish out of water and that you are struggling to accept your new reality, but I just want to ask you something," she said. "Do you trust that he would never steer you wrong and never let you down? Is that enough for you?"

I maintained eye contact with my mother in law but didn't open my mouth to respond. Of course I trusted him. I trusted him with my heart and my life, but I was still trying to figure out if that was enough. Sophia smiled and rubbed my cheek again.

"You don't have to answer me right now, Mi amor," she said. "Just please try to find that answer for yourself. If the answer is yes, come back to your family. Come home. He may not say it to you directly, but your husband is lost without you."

I nodded in response.

"Well," Sophia said, kissing me on the cheek before standing up. "Let's go see your babies. I know you've been dying to see them much like they've wanted to see you."

CAMERON

I sat on the edge of the bed and pulled off my boots. After releasing a tired sigh, I unbuttoned my work shirt, pulled it off, and tossed it onto the floor next to my shoes. I rubbed my hands over my face. It had been a long and tiring day. Since my release, my father had me working at the family-owned body shop. I originally thought that it would be more of a supervisory role where I mostly did paperwork and told other people what to do. I was wrong. Although I had a management title, my father actually had me doing real work. After high school, I had completed a program to become a certified automotive technician. He said that if we were going to own such a business someone should actually know how to work in the business. I was starting to wonder if he was preparing me for a life outside of the drug business all along. Typical Julian Reid to make sure that all bases were covered, and I had something to fall back on.

It had been almost four months since I got back home, and I still had not adjusted to my new life. Without my mother's knowledge I started working with my father when I was sixteen years old. Not being associated with the business was foreign territory for me. I didn't like it one bit. I was also still staying at my father's house, which worked for the time being, but I planned to get my own place soon. The house was definitely big enough for the both of us, but I had lived on my own since I was eighteen. Also while my father's love life was flourishing for the first time since my mother passed, I had not put forth much effort into rejoining the dating scene. Not seriously anyway. I had been out a few times here and there, but I wasn't pursuing any of the women seriously. Despite our drama and the actions that led to our demise, I missed Shannon terribly.

I heard my father's footsteps coming down the hallway before I saw him appear in the open doorway of my bedroom.

"Long day?" he asked.

I looked up from my hands. "You could say that," I answered. "What you got going on?"

"Just got back from the YMCA. We had a back to school supply giveaway for the kids," he answered. "I'm about to get ready for dinner with Sandra in a little bit. You got any plans for this evening?"

I shook my head. "Not really," I admitted. "Might step out a little later and see what my partners have going on. Might not. I'm a little tired, to be honest. I guess my body is still getting used to doing real physical work."

My father stepped inside of my room and leaned against the wall.

"I know you're still getting used to the way that things are right now, but I hope you can see that everything is working out for the best."

"That's what you honestly think?" I asked.

He nodded. "Yes, I do," he said. "To be honest, I was tired. Tired of running the game and the toll it had taken on me and our family. We lost your brother and almost lost your sister. You almost lost your freedom. I had to think about if it was all worth it or not, and I didn't think so. Now we all have the rest of our lives ahead of us. I'm still running a business, but in another way. Your sister is adjusting to her life as a wife and a mother, and you ... you get to reclaim your life as well."

"In what way? You and PO pretty much decided my fate at the request of Aaron and his father."

"True, and don't get me wrong it was for the benefit of the business," he said, "but also what was best for you."

I smirked. "Yeah okay."

"No. Seriously. You were forced into a life and down a path that I don't think was a good fit for you," he answered. "Now you get to build a life and future that's independent of my career choices and the name that I built for myself. You get to create a name for yourself whether it's in the automotive industry or as a small business owner yourself. Separating you from the drug game is probably going to be one of the best things I ever did for you."

I shrugged my shoulders. "Maybe."

I had been looking down at my boots, but I looked back up at my father to see a slight grimace on his face.

"Are you okay?"

"Yeah," he nodded. I watched as he rubbed his upper arm. "Feeling a little under the weather, but I'm good."

"You sure?"

My father nodded and smiled. "Of course. Your old man's as strong as an ox, and I've got dinner plans with my lady. A little lightheadedness isn't going to stop me from that," he said. "Probably did too much running around today at the Y. I'm going to get a glass of water and get myself ready for this steak I plan on eating tonight."

I laughed. "Alright. I feel you on that," I said. "A steak sure sounds good tonight. Maybe I'll call one of my new little lady friends and grab some dinner myself."

"Your more back to your old self than you realize," my dad laughed, as he turned to leave my room. He paused in the doorway. "Try and think about the things I said, Cam. You're a grown man, but you're still my baby boy. I only want the best for you. If you can learn to accept things for the way that they are, I think you'll be able to find happiness."

I shrugged my shoulders. "Maybe you're right, Pops. I guess we're going to see."

My dad nodded and exited my room. I laid back on my bed with the cell phone in my hand scrolling to see who I was going to invite to dinner.

AARON

The past several weeks had been stressful, to say the least. When Jada initially left, I didn't have time to really think about the reality of the situation. Work was busy. When I wasn't traveling from city to city checking on the operation, I was home helping my mother with my dad and his illness and taking care of the kids. With things starting to get back to a normal pace of business, I was starting to realize that my marriage might really be over. In six weeks, I had only seen her on FaceTime when she called to talk to the kids. Our conversations were minimal and forced, and we mostly only spoke about the children. To the best of my knowledge, she still had no idea if she wanted a life with me – a life that would require her to move to Miami.

I hated being at odds with her, but I had to take care of business. No one imagined that my father would fall ill and that I would have to take over for him so soon. I thought I would have time for Jada to adjust to our married life before I assumed the throne. However, my father was diagnosed with cancer, we got shot by Michaela Pitt, I had to disappear for months and now we were facing our current situation. The timing could not have been worse, but my father had been grooming me for this moment since I was eleven years old. What was I supposed to do?

I sat in the backseat of the rented large SUV with Luke while our driver pulled into traffic. We were originally scheduled to be in California for another day or so, but we concluded our business earlier. We would be heading back to Miami in the morning, and I couldn't wait to kiss my kids and sleep in my own bed. A wave of disappointment washed over me at the thought that my wife would not be there when I returned home. I picked up my cell phone and scrolled through my contacts. I hovered over Jada's name. I had half a mind to call her but ended up sitting the phone back on my lap and staring out of the window.

"What's on your mind, Black?" Luke's voice broke into my thoughts.

"Nothing man. Just ready to head home in the morning."

"Bullshit," Luke laughed, shaking his head at me. "We've been friends since grade school nigga. You know I know you."

I sighed in response.

"Are you going to call her?" Luke asked.

"Who?"

"Your wife."

I looked at my best friend and shook my head. "For what?"

"Because you miss her. That's obvious as hell to anyone who's been around you lately."

"So what?" I asked. "Of course I miss her, man. That doesn't change anything though. If things are going to improve, it has to be because she wants them to. It has to be what she wants. A late-night phone call telling her I miss her ain't gonna change shit."

This time Luke sighed. "Alright, man. Whatever," he said. "If you ain't gonna call her, let's at least do something about that funky ass mood you've been in."

I stared at my best friend with narrowed eyes. "Like what?"

There was a look of mischief on Luke's face that I was way too familiar with. It was the look that almost always ended up with one of us getting into trouble. Luke leaned forward towards Frank, our driver and part of our security.

Luke slapped Frank on the shoulder and said, "Change of plans, Chief. Instead of heading back to the hotel, why don't you take us on over to that club we passed earlier. Boss man needs a drink or two."

Frank nodded in acknowledgment and crossed a couple of lanes of traffic to change his course of direction. I looked at Luke.

"Bruh, I ain't really in the mood for all of that tonight. Let's just take it in and call it a night. It's already after midnight."

"You can sleep on the plane in the morning," Luke said, settling back into his seat.

I shook my head but decided not to put up a fight. I stared out of the window again while Frank continued our drive. When we pulled up to the busy nightclub, we quickly made our way inside. Frank and Eddie, the other part of our security, followed us into the club. When I was in Atlanta, I was able to move around more freely. When I was in Miami, and especially since taking over for my dad, I rarely made moves alone.

We surprisingly found an available section, and Luke ordered a couple of bottles of alcohol. Frank and Eddie didn't drink while they were working, and I knew there was no way Luke and I were going to drink all that alcohol. I decided to roll with it though. It was his money to waste. Half an hour later, I realized what my friend was doing. It was obvious he was trying to get me intoxicated. He was also trying to distract me with the several thirsty women he invited into our section for free drinks. I released a deep breath and leaned back against the leather cushions of the sofa.

I took a sip from my cup of liquor while I halfway listened to the woman that slid her way next to me. She had to have been talking for the last fifteen minutes or so, but I had no clue what she was saying. I only paid enough attention to add a couple of "oh yeahs" and "reallys" to make it seem like I was interested in her conversation. She was attractive. She reminded me of Kara Ross – the last woman I dated before Jada. Hair styled perfectly, cute face, designer clothes hugging every curve of her body, but my mind was somewhere else. Luke's intent was to distract me from the issues in my personal life, but all I was thinking was how I would much rather be with my wife.

"Your friend said you all are not from here?" the woman said, leaning in so I could hear her clearly over the music.

"We're not."

"How long are you in town?"

"Headed out first thing in the morning."

She slid a little closer to me on the sofa until her thigh was pressed against mine. I looked around for Luke and shook my head when I saw he was already tipsy and chatting up some chick with his arm draped around her shoulders.

"You trying to end the night here or you want to have a different type of fun before you leave town?" she asked.

I lowered my glass and looked at her. A few years ago, she wouldn't have had to say anything else. Before I met Jada, I would have been on my way out of the club with the attractive woman sitting next to me. A few years ago, Luke wouldn't have had to force me to go to the club. However, the days of my past were over. Although my marriage was hanging on by a thread, I didn't want to leave the club with the fine ass woman sitting next to me. I just wanted to go home.

Before I could respond to her, I felt my phone vibrating in my pocket. I pulled my phone out, frowning in confusion when I saw Vanessa's name on my screen. I had no idea why she would be calling me at that time of night. Thinking it must have been a mistake I let it go to voicemail and looked back at the woman who was trying to take me home. I opened my mouth to respond to her proposition but stopped when my phone started vibrating again. It was Vanessa for a second time.

"Excuse me," I said to the woman. "I need to answer this."

I stood up abruptly and headed for the exit. Eddie followed me while Frank stayed with Luke. It was after four o'clock in the morning in Atlanta, if Vanessa was trying to get ahold of me something was wrong – most likely with my wife. Before I could reach the curb outside the front door, the call went to voicemail. However, Vanessa started calling me again. I answered as soon as I stepped outside of the door.

"Vanessa, what's going on?"

"I know it's late. I'm sorry to bother you. I just didn't know if Jada had called you."

"Called me about what?"

"She was really upset, and she rushed out of the house. I don't even know if she has her phone with her."

"What is she upset about, Vanessa?"

"I was at the condo with her and your mom, because I wanted to see the kids. But then she got a phone call ..."

My mom and my kids? I had no clue what Vanessa was talking about. I had no idea why my mother or my children would be in Atlanta. *Was something wrong with them?* I could tell Vanessa was upset as well, but I needed her to get to the point.

"Vanessa, is something wrong with my kids?"

"No. No. The kids are fine. It's Julian."

"Julian?" I asked even more confused than before. "Vanessa, what the hell is going on?"

"He had a heart attack when he was at dinner with his girl-friend," Vanessa said. "It's not looking good at all. He's on a ventilator, and Jada is a mess. I know you two aren't in a great place, but I just ... I just thought ... "

"No. I understand, Ness. I appreciate you calling me," I said, shaking my head. "Is my mother still there?"

"No. She left for the airport when Jada and I headed to the hospital."

"Alright, Ness. Stay with her as long as the hospital will allow. I'm in California right now, but I'll get to Atlanta as soon as I can. Let me know of any updates."

"Okay."

I ended the call and shook my head as I stood on the sidewalk outside the club. Eddie looked at me with concern.

"Boss, is everything okay?"

I shook my head. "Nah man. It's not. I need you to get Luke and Frank," I answered him. "I gotta get to Atlanta."

JADA

After hours of tests and consults with different physicians, it had come to this. I stood in the hospital room numb – completely void of emotion. For once, I actually understood what people meant when they referenced having an out-of-body experience. I was there, present in that room, but it did not feel like it. I felt like I was outside of myself watching the situation unfold. The doctor and nurses moved about doing what they needed to do until the critical machines and monitors were disconnected. I don't know how much time passed, but I watched and listened as the vital monitor flatlined. Ayanna stood on the other side of the room crying heavily as Tony rubbed her back in an effort to console her. The medical staff called the time of death and said a few other things before quietly leaving the room. Tony responded. I couldn't really process anything that had been said.

I was having a hard time processing anything. It took a few moments before I even remembered to breathe. None of this felt real. None of the prior twenty-four hours of my life even made sense. This wasn't supposed to be happening. Manny Mercer had been the sick father, not mine. Manny had been the one we were all concerned about while he battled his cancer diagnosis. My father had been the textbook picture of strength and liveliness. So, I was having quite a great deal of trouble accepting the fact that my father was laying lifeless in the hospital bed in front of me.

"Jada?" Tony called to me. His voice sounded a lot farther away than the other side of the room. "Did you hear me?"

I hadn't.

I turned to look at him and shook my head.

"I said that Yanni and I can finish taking care of things here," he said. He paused. "Are you okay to drive home?"

I paused. Home. Home? What did that word even mean anymore? Nothing felt like home to me. Although I fought to hold on to the condo, it didn't feel like home anymore. The house in Sandy Springs was gone, and I had not been to Miami in several weeks. My life in Atlanta felt nothing like I had been used to, and I had not fully committed to a life in Miami. What the hell was *home*?

"I'm fine."

Tony's eyes lowered to my hands. My eyes followed. I didn't realize how tightly I was gripping my phone. I slightly relaxed my hands.

"Are you sure?" Tony asked. "I'm sure I can get Vanessa or someone up here to make sure you get home okay."

I shook my head. "No. It's okay, but I am going to get out of here. Make sure someone calls Cameron."

Tony nodded in agreement. I leaned in to give him a quick hug, and I kissed my sister on the cheek before exiting the room. I paused in the hallway for a brief moment, leaning against the wall for support. My head was spinning, and I felt like I was going to throw up. I shut my eyes tightly and took in a sharp, deep breath. After that moment passed, I made my way out of the hospital and into my truck.

I don't remember the drive home but several minutes later I

pulled into a parking space in the deck at my condo. I shut the engine off and sat there for a minute before exiting. It was starting to get dark outside, but I had a feeling that I wouldn't be getting any sleep that night. I grabbed my things and made my way into my building, entering on the ground floor. The concierge spoke to me as I made my way through the lobby, but I don't know what he said either. I was numb and in a daze as I pressed the elevator button to take me to the twelfth floor.

When I reached my door, I pulled out my key and turned the lock, letting myself into my darkened condo. I immediately noticed that the doors to my balcony were open. Quickly, I reached to flip on the nearest light switch. There was a large bouquet of red roses on the kitchen island. I made my way towards the balcony. Aaron's back was towards me as he stood watching the city below. I paused in the doorway and placed a hand on the frame of the door to steady myself.

After not feeling anything for the minutes and hours previously, a rush of emotions hit me, and I was feeling everything all at once. The tightness in my chest was overwhelming. Aaron turned towards me with his hands in his pockets. His eyes mirrored the sadness in mine. At the sight of my husband's face, my chest heaved up and down uncontrollably as I struggled to catch my breath. Aaron quickly made his way over to me, pulling me into his arms.

"You're ... here ..." I said in between ragged breaths and my pouring tears.

"There's nowhere else that I would be right now, mama."

He kissed my face and used his thumbs to wipe away my tears.

"My dad ... he's ... he's ..."

"Sssssshhhh," Aaron said, pulling me into his chest. "I know, mama. It's going to be okay."

I tried to relax in his embrace, allowing my head to rest against his chest. In that moment, I wasn't sure if I truly believed that anything would ever be okay again. However, I felt assured that whether it was or wasn't, Aaron would be by my side. Since the moment we met, and even when I fought against it, Aaron had always been there for me. With the recent events between us, I couldn't for the life of me understand why.

After a few moments of resting in his arms, I pulled back so I could look into his eyes.

"I'm sorry about the way I left Miami," I said. "I'm so sorry … for everything."

He shook his head. "We ain't even got to get into all of that tonight," he said. "Let's just head inside."

I allowed Aaron to lead me into the condo and into the bedroom. Surprisingly, it did not take long for me to fall asleep by his side.

The next few days were a blur. I was present, but Ayanna made most of the decisions. Luke was in communication with Manny and handling most of the day to day business which allowed Aaron to be by my side since the night I came home from the hospital. The kids were in Miami in Sophia's care. Ayanna had assured me that she was in contact with Cameron, but he had not been around. At least he had not been in the same place at the same time as me. I actually had not seen my brother since the day of AJ's birthday party in Atlanta. I had hoped that our conflict would resolve itself over time.

It turned out I was wrong.

Until my relationship with Aaron turned serious, Cameron and I had always been close. We had been best friends and each other's protectors – even more so after the death of our mother. It was hurtful to not be able to lean on each other in one of the most difficult points in my life.

I stood in the doorway of the kitchen, leaning against the frame as people passed me offering their condolences. We were at the repass after my father's funeral. Ayanna had chosen to have the meal at a local community center where our father donated a lot of time and money. There were so many people coming and going trying to speak to me that I was regretting not having a smaller, more private memorial.

As I looked around the facility, my eyes rested on Cameron. He was standing there dressed in an all-black suit. He did not ride with the family to the church. With the size of the crowd, I had no idea if he had been at the funeral, but at least he was at the repast. He was standing with PO and a group of other men who had worked for my father, casually sipping his drink and looking stressed. His eyes wandered around the room before resting on me. Our eyes remained fixed on each other while he excused himself from the group of men. Arms folded at my waist, I nervously toyed with my wedding rings while my brother made his way over to me.

"I didn't see you at the church."

My voice was low enough to not be heard by anyone passing by.

"I was there. Out of the way in the back."

"Out of the way? Cameron, we are family. What the hell?"

Cameron shrugged his shoulders and took a sip of his drink. I sighed heavily and shook my head.

"Where have you been?"

"Minding my business," he said. His jaw was tight. "You don't need to know about my whereabouts. Ain't shit changed between us just because Pops is gone. You and me ain't cool."

I sucked my teeth at him. "Then what the hell did you walk over here for?"

"Yanni said you might be spending some more time in Atlanta. I just wanted to make sure that you and I have a clear understanding."

"Oh yeah? And what is that?

"Your assistance is not needed with any of the family busi-nesses just because that nigga you married revealed himself to be the fuck nigga I always thought he was and you ran home to escape."

I folded my arms a little tighter and let out a slow, deep breath. I hesitated. Taking a moment to calm myself, I glanced down at the So Kate Louboutins on my feet before I looked back into my brother's face. I shook my head at him again.

"Now is not the time for this shit, Cameron."

"Yeah alright," he said with a smirk as he took another sip of his drink. His forehead wrinkled into a frown right as I felt Aaron beside me, placing his hand on the small of my back and kissing my forehead. Cameron looked me directly in my eyes as he said, "As long as we have an understanding, we're good. You chose your side. Stay your ass over there."

"You good, mama?" Aaron asked me quietly.

I nodded in response, avoiding eye contact with either of them. Cameron took a step towards us, but Aaron raised a hand to prevent him from getting any closer to me.

"We're having a private family conversation," Cameron said to Aaron. "Shit don't concern you, bruh."

"And I see that you still haven't gotten it through your head that your sister is and will always be my concern," Aaron said. His voice was firm. "If y'all need to have some conversation to air some shit out, you can do that shit some other time when we're in another space. This ain't it ... *bruh.*"

"I don't need your permission to speak to her," Cameron challenged.

Aaron laughed and shook his head. "Knock it off with the tough guy shit, Cam," he said. "You and I both know how I get down. You've gotten by with me on the strength of your father's name and your blood relation to my wife. Your daddy can't save you, and you're rubbing your sister the wrong way. You and I would be having a totally different *conversation* right now if it was a different time and place."

My eyes cut towards Aaron. I knew that there was tension

between the two of them, but Aaron had never directly threatened Cameron in my presence. I turned my attention towards my brother. Both his jaw and his fists were clenched. He took another sip of his drink and then walked away without commenting any further.

Much later that evening, Aaron and I finally made it back to my condo. I walked in and immediately kicked my heels off by the door. Aaron walked in behind me, locking the door and setting the alarm.

"I gotta get out of this dress. Can you unzip me?" I asked quietly, as I pulled my hair up from my neck.

Aaron unzipped my black Stella McCartney dress and kissed my cheek. I turned to face him.

"I think I need a hot bath ... care to join?"

Aaron nodded. I slipped my hand inside his and led us to the bathroom. Minutes later, we were relaxing in the soaker tub – my head against his chest and his arms wrapped around my shoulders.

I closed my eyes and sighed. "I'm calling my real estate agent Monday morning," I said, breaking the quiet between us. "I'm putting the condo on the market. I'm done with Atlanta."

Aaron was quiet for a few moments before asking, "Are you sure?"

I nodded. "I don't know what I was trying to hold onto," I said. "There's nothing here for me anymore. Not anything worth being separated from my family."

Aaron was quiet again. Then he let out a deep sigh of his own.

"Look, mama, I'm sorry for the way I spoke to you before you left Miami," he said. "There's been so much going on, but I shouldn't have used that tone with you. Jada, I love you, and I want our family back together. I want to get on the other side of whatever this dark cloud is that's been hanging over us. I just want things to get back to the way they were before."

"I don't know if things will ever get back to how they were before," I said, "but that doesn't mean that they won't get better. Aaron, I love you – so much. You being here for me the last few days with no distractions has meant the world to me. Very few people in this life have ever cared for me the way that you have."

"You're my rib, mama. I ain't right without you by my side," he said. "I miss you. The kids miss you, but if you're going to come back, I want it to be for the right reasons – not just because you're grieving."

"It's not just the grief talking. The past few days have really opened my eyes to the fact that my father was right about you from the start. I'm in good hands. All the love I need is with you and the family that we've built. I trust that you won't ever lead me wrong or let me down. Baby, there are a lot of reasons why I want to come home," I said. I took his hands and moved them down to my stomach. "… and one very important reason."

Aaron hesitated. "What are you saying, mama?" he asked for clarification.

"With everything that was going on between us I didn't want to say anything until I was completely sure, but I went to the doctor the other day," I answered. "I'm pregnant … nine weeks along."

"Jada, are you serious?"

I nodded. "Very … and my doctor said everything looks good so far."

Aaron wrapped both arms around me, hugging me tightly. He kissed my cheek. "Damn mama … I'm happy as fuck … but I can't say that I'm surprised," he said. "You ain't been able to keep your hands off of me."

I playfully slapped his hand, and we both laughed. I settled back into Aaron's arms, savoring our moment of togetherness.

EPILOGUE

ONE MONTH LATER

JADA

I nodded in response to whatever the mover said, but I hadn't been paying too much attention to the words that were coming out of his mouth. I signed the forms on the clipboard he held in front of me. All I knew was that he said something about my things being in Miami by the end of the week before he handed me a business card if I had any questions.

I smirked and shook my head as he walked away. Of course, I had questions but none of them were related to the physical aspects of my move. With my hands on my hips, I sighed as I looked around the living area of my near-empty condo. There were two guys with the moving company grabbing the last few boxes. I grabbed a bottle of water from the kitchen island and headed to the balcony. The balcony was almost empty as well as all that remained was two outdoor folding chairs and a small table. I lowered myself into one of the chairs, propping my feet up on the railing in front of me.

What am I doing? I asked myself as I took a sip from the bottle of water. So much had happened in the last three years. Never in a million years would I have pictured the current state of my life. After retiring from the drug game at the beginning of the year, my father died from a sudden heart attack just as he was starting to enjoy his new life. My older brother was also dead – a casualty of the war with Caleb Bridges and KS9 – and my younger brother said I was dead to him. I took another sip of my water and shook my head. The state of my relationship with Cameron still hurt a great deal. My sister and I had surprisingly grown close, but now I was about to move away and turn my Atlanta businesses over to her control. I was leaving Atlanta, the only home I had ever known, to move to Miami to be with my family and work on my marriage. I was a wife and a mother – something I always wanted. I just never figured it would happen the way that it did.

If someone asked me five years ago, what my life would look like now, my prediction would have been drastically different from my reality. Just a couple of days away from my thirtieth birthday, I would have thought I would be married to Israel Mann with at least two children – maybe one on the way. We would be thriving professionally, surrounded by the love and support of our families. Thinking about that actually made me laugh out loud. I had not spoken to Israel since running into him at the mall when I was seven months pregnant with AJ when he was getting ready for his engagement party. His wedding to Angelina was covered by various gossip blogs and magazines and rumor had it they were expecting their first child. I, on the other hand, was preparing for my second child with my husband – the head of an international multimillion-dollar criminal empire.

I took another sip of my water and set the bottle down on the table. I heard movement behind me and looked over my shoulder to see Vanessa joining me on the balcony.

"Come. Have a seat," I motioned towards the empty chair next to me.

Vanessa's face was tight with frustration as she sat down.

"So, you're really going to do this?"

I signed. "Ness, please. Don't start, okay? You always knew there was a possibility that we would live in Miami."

"I mean, sure. In the back of my mind I knew that his business was rooted in Miami," she started, "but I didn't think that you would be selling your place and going down there after everything that has happened."

"He's my husband, Vanessa. You're married now. I don't know why you can't understand this."

"Husband or not … that doesn't change all the things he did."

I shrugged my shoulders. "He did what he had to do."

"He lied to you and faked his death for over six months. He had one of your friends killed, sold your house with little to no discussion, and put your brother out of work … I mean come on!" she exclaimed. "The list of his controlling acts and deception just go on and on."

"Everything he's done has been for the sake of our family and my livelihood. Michaela Pitt was not going to stop until we were six feet under. He did what he needed to do to protect us and eliminate her. Shannon …" my voice trailed off as I looked away, breaking my eye contact with my best friend. "Shannon, did it to herself, Ness. She allowed her anger to turn her to take Cameron and maybe the whole family down. We couldn't allow that."

I bit my lip to keep the emotion out of my voice before I continued.

"Cameron is out of jail now. That's what matters most. The fact that he has his freedom is what's important. He can run the family businesses in my father's absence. With all the money my dad left behind, Cam will never have to worry about finances," I explained. "His actions over the last few years have shown that he's not cut out for the life that he was trying to live."

"Are you?" Vanessa snapped.

"Am I what?"

"Are you cut out for the life that you're trying to live?" Vanessa asked. "The Jada that I know would have never allowed someone to drive a wedge between her and her beloved baby brother. The Jada that I know is caring and compassionate and would have never looked me in the face and said that Shannon did it to herself. I'm not sure I know who you are anymore."

"Were we supposed to let Shannon ruin everything just because she was in her feelings? If you really know me, you know that my family comes first – always. That includes the Mercers now. I love Cameron, but in a matter of months he put his family in a position to lose everything that our father and the Mercers spent years building. His arrogance and immaturity could have cost my father and my husband their freedom," I responded. "Cameron has to know that. He'll come around eventually."

"And what if he doesn't? He said you were dead to him."

"Then tough shit," I said, shrugging my shoulders. "That's his choice. His loss. I did nothing wrong. He could still be sitting in a federal prison. He owes his freedom to my husband. I am pregnant, Vanessa. I can't waste my energy on a grown ass man who refuses to accept responsibility for his own actions. If he cared so much about Shannon, he would have never been fucking that goddamn DEA agent in the first place."

"Wow," Vanessa said. She rose to her feet and leaned against the balcony's railing, facing the street below. After a moment of silence between us, she turned around to face me. "One could say that if Aaron really loved you, he wouldn't –"

"See that's what we're not going to do," I said, jumping to my feet. "What we're not going to do is question his love for me. People have said a lot of things about DJ and his indiscretions, and I never disrespected you by repeating those things to your face. You chose a life with him, and I respect that. I just need you to do the same for me."

Vanessa stared at me hard but didn't respond.

"Vanessa, this is my life now. This is the decision that I have made. Why can't you just be happy for me?"

"Are you happy?" she asked.

I frowned.

"Are you really happy, Jada? Because you don't look like it. I haven't seen the light in your eyes since the first time you held your son. You know why it's so easy for you to support me and DJ? Because I'm actually happy. Can you say the same?"

I frowned. "Vanessa, no one can be happy all day every day."

"That's not what I asked you. I didn't ask if you were happy all day every day. Are you happy with your life right now?"

I didn't respond. I was starting to get frustrated with our conversation.

"That's what I thought," she said. "This is not the life you pictured for yourself. You've become the very type of woman you said you never wanted to be."

"It may not be the life I pictured, but it's the life that I have," I answered. "I love Aaron, and I know that he loves me too. Every relationship goes through rough patches, and we're working through it."

Vanessa smirked. "Well, I hope it all works out, friend. Good luck in Miami."

I stood there in silence and watched as my best friend strolled back through my condo and out the front door. I let out a deep sigh. *So much for warm farewells.* Cameron still wasn't speaking to me and Vanessa had shown her displeasure with my decision as well. So much was changing for all of us, but I still felt confident with my choice. Whether or not I had the support of some of those closest to me, I was still headed to Miami to reunite my family for good.

After a few more moments in my empty condo, I called Danny up to help me with my bags. We made our way down to the truck and then on to the airport. A few hours later, we arrived at Miami International Airport, where Julio was already waiting to take us to our next destination. Julio helped Danny with the bags before we all climbed into the truck. I settled back into my seat, scrolling through my social media accounts. Several minutes into our ride, my phone vibrated with a text message from Aaron.

"See you soon, mama. Love you"

I smiled and texted him back. *"Love you too, baby. See you soon"*

Several minutes into the ride Julio made a left when he should have made a right, and I looked on in confusion. I sat back quietly wondering if he was taking a short cut to the Mercers that I was unaware of. However, minutes later, I realized that we were headed in an entirely different direction than the home belonging to Manny and Sophia Mercer.

"Hey, Julio ... where are we going?" I asked. "This doesn't look like the way to the estate."

"No ma'am it's not. Aaron is at another location and asked me to bring you there," he answered.

I trusted Julio so I wasn't too alarmed, and Danny looked relaxed as if he was also aware of the change in plans. Still, I opened my messaging app and asked Aaron where he was. He responded telling me that he was waiting for me and would see me soon. I relaxed again knowing that whatever was going on Danny, Julio, and Aaron were all in on it. A short while later we drove through a pricey residential area with Julio navigating the truck to a security gate. After gaining access to the property, Julio continued down a narrow path surrounded by picture perfect landscaping that led to a beautiful three-story water-front mansion. Julio pulled into the driveway and killed the engine.

"Where are we?" I asked.

"Come on," Julio said. "I'll show you."

Danny opened my door and helped me out of the vehicle. I followed them to the front door of the house, which was unlocked. Julio led us into the house and towards the back. The fully furnished home looked brand new, and I could smell the faint aroma of fresh paint. When we reached the double glass doors leading to the back yard, my eyes opened wide. Olivia, Aaron, and AJ were playing and running around the huge outdoor space.

Julio and Danny hung back while I walked closer. I opened the door, catching Aaron's attention. He looked in my direction and smiled while the kids rushed towards me. I scooped AJ up into my arms and hugged Olivia back when she wrapped her arms around my waist. Aaron crossed the yard and kissed my lips.

"Welcome home," he said.

"Home?"

Aaron slipped his hands into his pockets while his lips pulled into his usual half smile. "Yeah, mama. It's finally finished. Welcome to our new home," he said. "Consider it an early birthday present."

"Wow," I said with a surprised smile. "How did you keep this from me?"

Aaron shrugged his shoulders. "I have to keep a few tricks up my sleeve. I've gotta keep you on your toes."

"I'm speechless. I love it."

"I love you," he said, kissing me again. He placed a hand on my baby bump and said, "I'm excited to start this new chapter with our family under the same roof in a place that you can call home. You've done so much to prove that you're committed to our marriage and our life now. The least I could do is give you a place of your own. A little piece of Miami that belongs to you."

I leaned into Aaron, placing my hands on both sides of his

face before kissing his lips. When I pulled away, Aaron smiled and took my hand.

"Now come on so I can show you around."

Aaron Mercer never ceased to amaze me. Just when I felt like I was giving up so much in Atlanta, I realized that I was gaining so much more in Miami. My family. Our home. I was finally ready to accept all that came along with being married to him. I was ready to leave Atlanta behind and start my life in Miami as Mrs. Jada Mercer – wife to the head of the Ramirez Cartel. I knew that none of our problems would be solved overnight, but I also knew that there was no denying that we belonged together. I finally felt at home.

THANK YOU

Cole Hart
SIGNATURE NOVELS

To our loyal Cole Hart Signature readers,

Cole Hart Signature is always growing and changing. Some of you have been following Cole Hart since the beginning of his career, while others have seen us go from Cole Hart Presents to Cole Hart Signature. Then there are our daily new supporters who've only known us for what we are as a company today. Despite our changes, how or when you became a fanatic, we want to kindly thank you for the support.

We appreciate all our Cole Hart Readers because without every single one of you, we wouldn't be the company we are today.

If this book is your first introduction to our company, welcome! And be sure to sign up for email list by click the link, http://bit. ly/2BtGCXH, and joining out text-mail list by texting Cole-HartSig to (855)231-5230. Cole Hart Signature also has a Facebook group where fans get to discuss the plot, characters, overall releases about their favorite book. If itching for new and interesting conversation, click the link, https://geni.us/ColeHartSignatureRead, to join today!

Lastly, Cole Hart Signature is always interested in partnering with aspiring authors, new or experienced, who thrive in the African Urban Fiction and Romance Fiction genre. If you're interested in joining our team, go to www.colehartsignature.com/submissions.

Once again, we truly appreciate all the support over the years.

Much Love,
    CHS

ACKNOWLEDGMENTS

As always, thank you to my family and closest friends. You all have been in my corner encouraging me from the beginning. Collectively, you gave me confidence to share my stories with the world. You all mean everything to me.

To everyone who has read any of my work, thank you! It still feels surreal to get emails from readers asking when the next book is coming out, but I love all the support and interactions. Let's stay connected because more books are on the way!

ABOUT THE AUTHOR

Michelle Elaine is an author of African American and Urban fiction and romance. Born and raised in Atlanta, GA, she still resides in the metro area with her husband and sons. She has always been passionate about storytelling and character creation/development. This passion led to several short stories and development of plots and characters before she completed her first book, "A Good Girl & A Down South Millionaire". Visit her website and join her mailing list to stay in the know on the latest releases, etc.

Other ways to stay connected:
    Facebook – Author Michelle Elaine
    Instagram – authormichelleelaine
    Website – www.michelleelainebooks.com
    Email – michelleelainebooks@outlook.com

CPSIA information can be obtained
at www.ICGtesting.com
Printed in the USA
LVHW021542061120
670969LV00010B/984

9 798681 824237